BEST
LESBIAN EROTICA
OF THE YEAR

VOLUME TWO

BEST
LESBIAN EROTICA
OF THE YEAR

VOLUME TWO

Edited by
SACCHI GREEN

CLEiS
PRESS

Published in the United States by Cleis Press, an imprint of Start Midnight, LLC, 101 Hudson Street, Thirty-Seventh Floor, Suite 3705, Jersey City, NJ 07302.

Printed in the United States.
Cover design: Scott Idleman/Blink
Cover photograph: iStock
Text design: Frank Wiedemann
First Edition.
10 9 8 7 6 5 4 3 2 1

Trade paper ISBN: 978-1-62778-254-8
E-book ISBN: 978-1-62778-255-5

"Shaved," by Pascal Scott, is an excerpt from *Hard Limits* by Pascal Scott (Blackout Books, 2017).

CONTENTS

INTRODUCTION

The *Best Lesbian Erotica* series has been making our pulses pound now for twenty-two years. Some girls who weren't even born back then are old enough now to read erotica—and to write it. The title has changed, beginning with the 20th Anniversary Edition—this year's is *The Best Lesbian Erotica of the Year Volume 2*—but the aim is the same: to present the best lesbian erotic short stories of recent years. "Best," that is, in the eye (and imagination, and sensual responses) of the beholder. For an anthology it also means not only the best-written work, but the most varied, intriguing, downright hot stories that can be fit together in one balanced, absorbing book.

The choices are, of course, entirely subjective on the part of the editor, so here are just a few hints as to what pushed my buttons this year. The settings range from a Korean restaurant to the Mojave Desert to a comic book store to a silent-movie theater. The protagonists are all ages, from young students to seasoned self-identified dykes to elders whose fires still burn fiercely. You can find love and romance, power exchange, over-the-top sex toys, a superheroine, a Prohibition-era detective, and much more. And, of course, there is sex as varied and vivid as the settings and characters: explicit, often inventive, sometimes transformative, always steamy. Each story is distinctive in its way. Don't try to swallow too many all at once; take time to savor your favorites. Getting there is half the fun.

So what pushes your buttons? I hope you'll find it here, and even discover buttons you didn't know you had. Or zippers. Zippers are hot, too. Variety can be the spice of lust.

Sacchi Green
Amherst, MA

SIX DATES

A. D. Song

On their fifth date, Jesse took Nina to a tiny Korean restaurant tucked between a hair salon and a drug store. Smoky scents of meat and *ban chan*—side dishes—rose hot and heavy in the air. If Jesse closed her eyes and inhaled the fumes, she could imagine her parents' restaurant in the Koreatown back in Midtown Manhattan. Her mother would be manning the kitchen ferociously, punctuating each barked statement with a crack of her ladle. Her soft and steady father, eyes creased in quiet good humor, would be nudging Jesse, who waitressed more often than not, toward the customers spilling through the door, hungry for bowls of searing, spicy *kimchi jiggae* despite the summer heat. Koreans believed hot soups were perfect for hot nights, something Jesse carried with her despite moving across the country to her new job in Los Angeles.

They sat at a corner table, as Jesse always preferred when she was making her moves. And she would have to use every single one of them on Nina.

Nina kept Jesse on her toes, and had done so since they met along the aisle of colorful, multi-shaped dildos at the queer sex store where Nina worked. The first glance Jesse gave Nina was because, like Jesse, Nina was Korean; the second was because of Nina's fluid but fierce femininity.

With a pierced brow and limbs covered with an array of fine-lined, black-and-gray tattoos, Nina was tiny and graceful, even in her ridiculous, fat-heeled platform boots. She was as delicate as a music-box ballerina, complete with long black hair ribboning down her back in loose curls.

When Jesse found her stocking the bunny vibrators, Nina pretended not to notice her.

"Come here often?" Jesse asked.

Nina looked down at her name tag and looked back up, cocking her head ironically.

"Only on Tuesdays, Wednesdays, and Fridays."

"Great." Jesse smiled, leaning against the boxes of Vibratex Pearl Thunders. She knocked the turquoise one over. "Now I know where to find you."

Nina laughed and when Jesse asked her out, Nina swept her heavy, hooded eyes over this new specimen—from Jesse's short, sharp pompadour to the tips of her combat boots. Nina said, playfully, lightly, "We'll see," and gave a twinkling little smile full of promise and sin. And with that, Jesse was smitten.

Jesse did take her out, to an old movie theater, a record store, and a punk show. Despite—or because of—her job at the sex store, Nina claimed she was a traditional girl and refused to even kiss Jesse until they'd had six dates.

"Why six?" Jesse asked.

"It's a proper number."

"Oh, come on," Jesse protested. "Come on, you're really telling me I can't even give you a tiny"—she backed Nina slowly against a wall—"little"—she lowered her head until her mouth skimmed a breath above hers—"kiss?"

Nina knocked Jesse a full step back, with both her hands and the power of those dark eyes.

"No!" she snapped. She was smiling a little but still held firm. "Six dates."

Jesse had tried. But even when she made her moves on her against walls and into dark corners—and once on Jesse's bed, using her four-inch height advantage—Nina refused to be seduced. Even when Jesse kissed along the curve of her plant-stem-slender neck, making Nina shiver; even when Jesse smoothed her hands alongside Nina's sides and cupped her small breasts; even when Nina let Jesse stroke her outside her pants until their bodies were damp and trembling with desire, Nina would nudge her back and whisper, "Six dates."

And she would glide away—or roll away—with that unperturbed grace, trailing clouds of jasmine perfume and leaving Jesse very, very frustrated. And excited.

It was only their fifth date, but sitting at the corner table in this little Korean restaurant, Jesse sensed something was going to happen.

Nina wore red, a dark crimson the color of ripened plums. Her lips were painted the same color and they curved up now, teasingly, at Jesse. Nina had done something magical and feminine so that her eyes were smoky and her eyelashes long and black. There was a teasing female awareness in them, almost smug and entirely too aware of the havoc she was currently causing in Jesse's boxers. Something about that knowing femininity always fascinated and intrigued Jesse—even though, or maybe because, she wasn't born with it herself.

Nina leaned forward frequently so Jesse got a good eyeful of what she wore under her shirt—it was as red as her lips. Nina glanced at Jesse now and then, eyes bright, a small cat-smile curling her lips. She seemed excited, expectant, waiting for something. Entranced as Jesse was, she knew Nina would get whatever she wanted; Jesse's only power was how Nina would get it. Call it butches' intuition: Jesse was going to have her tonight.

She looked at Nina now, who sipped her barley tea.

"I'm surprised at you," Nina commented. "I didn't think we would come here."

"Would you have preferred a fancy French restaurant?"

"No, this is perfect. It's . . . us."

"Not quite." Jesse took Nina's hand, entangled their fingers. "Now it is."

The dark, rich raspiness of Nina's laugh tingled Jesse's skin.

They ate rice with platters of smoked meat, bowls of steaming soup, and small ceramic stone pots of steamed egg, all the while picking through side dishes of *kimchi*, seasoned spinach, boiled eggplant, and chunks of julienned white radish. They spoke of their families, Nina's part-time job at the sex store, and Jesse's time at the Culinary Institute.

And when Jesse mentioned the dessert she had made back at her apartment, Nina only said, "Why don't we do just that?" with a little smile.

After making their way to Jesse's apartment, Nina clapped as Jesse brought out the dessert.

"You made this?"

"I didn't just wait tables back in New York. I had to do something to graduate from the Culinary Institute."

It was a towering confection with mounds of cream, dotted with berries and shards of chocolate, dusted lightly with powdered sugar.

"It's beautiful. Thank you."

When Jesse offered a tiny, long-handled spoon, Nina merely said, "Feed me," and opened her mouth.

Willing to play along, Jesse fed Nina berries with cream, letting her slowly suck the cream off the spoon, watching her eyes close in pleasure as she savored each bite.

And when she leaned toward Jesse, offering her parted lips, still sticky with cream, Jesse only skimmed a berry along her lips and popped it into her mouth. Nina opened her eyes in surprise but Jesse merely said, "Let's take this to my room." Satisfied, Nina smiled and let Jesse sweep her into the bedroom.

Jesse cocked an eyebrow, unsurprised, when Nina took bondage cuffs out of her purse.

"My safeword is 'dessert,'" Nina told Jesse, her eyes gleaming in the settling darkness. With the shadows criss-crossing against her skin, she looked predatory and silkily beautiful, like some otherworldly creature, a feral hunt-ress, all sharp teeth and impossibly smooth skin.

Jesse grinned in response and took her time undressing Nina, letting the clothes fall off in achingly slow motion, and tying her up, cuffing her hands together.

As she finished, Jesse was awed by her date's beauty. Nina was proudly, defiantly naked—save for her panties— her ochre skin glowing in the slivers of silvery moonlight, all five feet of her stretched out on Jesse's black sheets.

Her hands were cuffed together, bound by black leather and silver chains, nestled into the sheets above her head. Her ankles were bound, knees pressed together and bent to one side, a teasing recourse to withhold her pussy from Jesse just a little bit longer. Jesse hovered inches above her body, relishing every spot their heated skin met in a light, magnetic touch.

"Kiss me," Nina breathed. Her lips were parted, ready. A lovely pink flushed her cheeks.

Jesse inhaled the musky scent of Nina's sweet pussy, her arousal already permeating the air. She was so incredibly wet, soaking through the thin, silky fabric of her red lace panties. Jesse looked at Nina, their eyes meeting hungrily in the dark. Nina, eager and impatient now that she'd started the game. Jesse, calm and still, her mind swiftly sliding into that dominant role, anticipating Nina's needs, her limits, and relishing, savoring the power.

"No."

Nina looked startled.

"It hasn't been six dates yet," Jesse pointed out.

At that, Nina cursed out loud, a string of invectives that could blister paint from the walls.

Jesse only narrowed her eyes, smiling a little. *Bratty little girl,* so used to guiding tops from the bottom, so accustomed to easily getting what she wanted. Well, she wasn't going to get that from Jesse. Instinctively, Jesse slid one hand under Nina's hip, the other hand grasping Nina's opposite shoulder. With a deft quickness and ease that caught Nina off guard, Jesse flipped Nina onto her stomach, pulling her up by her hips in one smooth, fluid motion so that she rested on her elbows and knees, ass thrust up in the cool night air.

Smack!

She spanked Nina across her small, round ass.

Nina half yelped, half moaned in response. Then, with a huff of outrage, she tried to twist around, trying to find purchase on the smooth sheets despite her bondage, wiggling deliciously in the process.

Smack!

Jesse smacked her across her ass again, just a touch harder than the first time.

"The first was for using bad language. This one is for questioning Daddy," Jesse said coolly.

Nina stilled, then turned her head and strained to look up at Jesse from her facedown position. Long strands of hair fell messily onto her face and pooled on the bed, as glossy black as raven feathers. Her pupils were dilated, her irises swallowed up by black. A hint of a smirk still lingered on her lips. She opened her mouth.

"Fuck you," she said.

With that, Jesse unlooped the belt from her jeans. Metal clinked against metal as she drew the leather out. Nina stilled when Jesse laid the belt firmly across her ass. Jesse could hear her breathing, soft catchy gasps of anticipation.

"Is that any way to talk to Daddy?" Jesse crooned.

Jesse pulled Nina's panties down roughly over her thighs, stopping to finger the sodden material. She wound the buckled end of the belt twice around her grip, and started out slow and steady, soft little love-taps against Nina's cheeks, pausing now and then to draw out the anticipation, the fear.

"Is that any way to talk to Daddy? Hmm?" Jesse repeated, swatting Nina's ass with one hand. She watched her asscheeks jiggle and sway in response. "Answer me."

When Nina gave no response, Jesse increased the force of her whipping, bringing the belt down and across Nina's ass faster and harder.

"Are you going to answer me, brat?"

Nina only grunted in response, her ass twitching, but otherwise staying resolutely silent and still. She was a proud little thing, the most dedicatedly stubborn brat. Considering her brassy fierceness, what else could she be? Nina's cheeks were tinged pink with embarrassment and arousal in equal parts, her wet panties still bunched at the crook of her knees. Jesse almost laughed out loud but kept a stern expression on her face.

Jesse began to smack her in earnest, drawing her arm back and putting her substantial strength into it. The belt whistled through the air and whipped Nina's ass in cracking snaps that echoed through the room. Nina started to make high-pitched little noises, breathy gasps melting into moans. Her ass started to glow, bright red welts rising against her skin. Jesse could see it flush even in the darkness.

Nina pressed her face down as the belt came down again, her cries muffled by the mattress. Her body started to jerk, no longer able to keep still.

"Stubborn brats are bad girls," Jesse hissed. "Daddy gets to do whatever he wants with a bad girl."

Jesse leaned over Nina's body, pressing down with enough force so Nina could feel her weight. She jerked Nina up a little and dipped a finger between her legs. Her pussy was so swollen and slick and wet, Jesse had to bite off a groan, clenching her teeth. Nina bucked her hips and tried to back onto Jesse's fingers, searching for friction.

"Oh no you don't." Jesse turned her head and bit Nina's ear roughly, tonguing it a little. Nina cried out in response.

Jesse got up, drew her arm back, and whipped Nina one last time with every ounce of strength she had. With that, Nina gave a deep shudder, her whole body collapsing onto the bed. She started to writhe, trying to relieve the burn that was surely spreading over her ass. She cried out, "No, Daddy. Daddy, please. Daddy . . . "

Jesse dropped the belt and rolled Nina gently back onto her back. She was no longer smirking; instead, tears gathered in the corners of her eyes, her lips puckered in a pout—the picture of a repentant little girl. A flood of tenderness and pride filled Jesse.

"What do we say to Daddy?" Jesse asked, softly, smoothing back Nina's rumpled hair.

"I'm sorry, Daddy. I'm sorry," she sniffled.

Jesse got her a glass of water, and let her drink from a straw.

"There's my girl," Jesse murmured. "You okay? You did so well. Good girl."

"Yes, Daddy. Daddy, please." Nina wiggled against her binds.

Jesse unbuttoned her jeans and pulled them off along with her boxers. She pulled on her harness, buckled it in and ran one hand over the length of her cock, but left her T-shirt and binder on. She released Nina from her restraints and let her massage her wrists.

"Get back on your knees."

When Nina got on her hands and knees, Jesse lubed up her cock and positioned it against Nina's entrance. Her pussy gleamed wetly, bare folds parting as she perked her ass up. Jesse eased slowly inside. Nina moaned deep in her throat as she rocked back, trying to take more of Jesse's cock.

Jesse rotated her hips, sliding around experimentally. Nina gasped, arching her back. She found that Nina liked it hard and fast, with short, rough strokes, and gave it as good as she was given, bouncing back on Jesse's cock wildly.

"See what you get when you're a good girl? You get what you want when you're a good girl." Jesse pumped harder, her hips slapping against Nina's ass. Their bodies smacked together.

"Yes, Daddy. Please, Daddy!" Her small hands clenched and unclenched on the blanket. Nina spread her legs wider and lifted up her ass, rocking back and forth faster and faster.

Nina was so wet, Jesse could hear slippery, squelching noises every time she slid inside her. Jesse ran her hands over Nina's body, cupping her small breasts, rubbing her hard nipples. She slipped two fingers inside Nina's mouth, and Nina sucked eagerly and fiercely, nipping them with her sharp, little teeth.

Jesse groaned, her own clit throbbing in response. She felt herself getting even wetter, if that was possible. Every inch of her skin felt hot and sensitive.

Jesse retrieved her wet fingers and reached around Nina's hip to rub her clit, still pounding into her from behind. Nina cried out louder, her whole body thrashing against the bed. Jesse could tell she was close by the way her pussy clenched around Jesse's cock.

Nina turned her head to the side as far as she could and whimpered, "May I come, Daddy?"

Jesse groaned when Nina asked. "Good girl." She pushed inside Nina harder and rubbed her clit faster. "Yes, you may come. Come for me, good girl. Come for me."

With that, Nina stiffened, her body suspended for seven, eight endless seconds, before finally starting to shake, her back arching with gasping, shuddering moans. She came in a hot gush of wetness, squeezing so hard against Jesse's cock that she pushed it out just a little. Jesse pumped slowly once, twice, before easing out gently when Nina's shudders abated.

Jesse let Nina go. She collapsed bonelessly onto the bed, ass still in the air. The marks were a faded pink, but still visible, making Jesse grin. Then, after collecting enough strength, Nina rolled onto her back and opened her sex-heavy eyes.

Breathing deeply, quivering slightly, tear-stained, she stretched like a satisfied cat, wrists flexing. Her red lipstick was smeared and half-gone, her hair mussed, like a beautiful, fucked-out vixen.

Jesse joined Nina on the bed. Faces close, foreheads knocking, their breath mingled. Jesse took Nina's face and, finally, kissed her red mouth. Nina's lips opened in invitation, yielding beneath Jesse's mouth, letting herself be claimed in the way butches need to claim. Nina's mouth was warm, her wet, small tongue twining with Jesse's for a quick moment before they broke free.

Jesse eased back, letting Nina nip at her bottom lip. She pulled Nina close, settling Nina's head on her shoulder, hair spilling everywhere. She breathed in the scent of Nina's apple shampoo, the smell of sex and sweat that still lingered in the air. It was quiet for a moment as they caught their breaths. Jesse was still wet, throbbing.

"What're we going to do for our sixth date?" Jesse asked, making Nina laugh out loud, bright and wicked and joyful.

"Oh, I can think of a few things." And with that, Nina pounced on Jesse and dragged her down.

ARM'S LENGTH

Theda Hudson

She was watching me again, pretending not to from her table beside the window. The light from the overhead fixture made a yellow pool on the table and she sat just outside of it.

What could a young thing like that, all hip and cool and lithe and lean with tits like little rosebuds—yes, I'd noticed—what could a little chickie like that want with a middle-aged dyke like me?

The cafe door opened. A cool breeze blew in the smell of rain to mix with the fresh-brewed coffee and ruffle my paper.

I stirred my mocha and lifted my éclair. When I took a bite, chocolate stuck to my lip and the sweet creamy filling spurted out. As I cleaned myself up, she stared at me, short, shaggy roan-colored hair falling over her forehead and across her right eye.

Trying for suavely wicked, I licked my lips and put the pastry to my mouth, tonguing it gently.

She stared at me like I was an alien from Mars and then, with one hand, flipped the book on the table closed. When she picked it up and stuffed it into the messenger bag hanging on the back of the faux vintage chair, I figured I'd shocked or insulted her.

Shrugging, I picked up my coffee and turned back to the paper folded neatly in quarters on the table. Kids these days. They think they're so sophisticated. When I refolded it to see the next page, I sensed movement and looked up to see her standing in front of me.

The light from the next table shone from behind her and I saw the outline of her sweet tits. I was filled with a sudden urge to put my arm around her hips, right above the waistband of those shabby-chic jeans, up under the edge of her shirt, and with my other hand, lift it so I could, oh so lightly, trace a finger up that little mound and circle her aureole until her nipple hardened.

Then I'd lean in, *oh,* set my mouth down on it and suckle softly. Until she arched into it, then I'd give her a nip and hold her still while I worked it over good, with plenty of teeth.

My pussy got hot and a little juicy just thinking about it. I squirmed a bit. Big Blue pressed against me, amplifying the pleasure.

But a sweet little chickie like her wouldn't want a dyke like me pawing her. She was probably going to chastise me for public lewdness. These kids today, so good at speaking their minds.

"Do you mind if I sit down here?"

I looked at her like she was some kind of Martian come down to Earth.

"Well, is this seat taken?" she asked, snarky as they come.

I regained my composure enough to shrug and gesture, "Go ahead."

She smiled so that her darling little bow lips opened enough to show a bit of tooth. Her two front teeth were a bit crooked. I imagined her mouth bruised and swollen from kissing. And those teeth running along my shoulder and the inside of my thighs.

"Did you hear me?"

I shook off the fantasy. "What?"

She sat down, scrunching her mouth up impatiently.

"I'm Toni Talbot. My friends call me TT."

TT, Titty? I smiled lewdly. What was this chickie doing at my table interrupting my coffee and paper ritual?

"My name's Louden." I'd given up my first name the day I left home and made it legal when I hit twenty-one. "What do you want?"

Suddenly this hip chick turned nervous. Was she here on a dare? I looked around to see who might be watching us.

"I want . . . " She twiddled with a ring on her right middle finger, an arty piece of twisted silver with tiny flecks of pink stone mixed into the strands. I wondered if she'd made it. She was artsy looking enough and the school was just around the corner.

I stared at her, remembering when my face was so innocent, so untried, so unbroken, so unworn. When my heart had not been broken and mended and girded. When my life looked bright and fresh and full of promise.

Where had all that gone?

I knew where: keeping a roof over my head while I chased my dreams and women and hopes. I'd gotten a few dreams at least.

"There's this girl," she said, leaning in conspiratorially.

Did she want to make her jealous? Hook me up?

How old was she anyway? Twenty-two, twenty-three? Young enough to be my kid if Barbara had won that argument. Really more a proposal. Either way, I'd refused, seeing only my parents, my own upbringing.

Barbara still sent cards at the holidays. She had three kids, a wife, a dog, and two cats. She was on the PTA, the homeowners association board, and drove a school bus.

I had a house, my studio, a reasonably long and respectably illustrious client list, and a cat that was supposed to be a mouser, but was more interested in a comfortable place to sleep.

"I really like her."

What did this kid's crush have to do with me? I looked down at my cup, the éclair, half-eaten, and the paper barely begun.

"And so?"

She whispered, "I have no idea what to do with her."

I tried to picture her fluttering around this girl, excited, puppy-love-struck, insecure, scared, and eager all at once.

Then I remembered my first sort of lover, a girl I went to school with. I took the lead and did the things I wanted to, learning as I watched to see how much she liked the way I touched her, the way I licked her pussy and sucked her tits. We drifted apart when she went for a boyfriend and I discovered art.

I picked up my cup and sipped, staring at this little slip of a woman who had a crush on some other woman. I wasn't sure if I felt hurt that it wasn't me or irked that she'd shared with me.

"And so, whaddya want from me?"

She sighed like I was dense. "You're a dyke. You're handsome. You know what to do with women."

I was handsome?

No one had ever told me I was beautiful or pretty, but Karen, my current sub, maintained I was good looking. I thought of her cuffed to the open frame at the Darker Wings club, her eyes glazed with pleasure, the apples of her ass red where I'd been at them with my gloved hand, the buffalo-hide flogger hanging over one shoulder, the falls tickling her tit.

Yeah, I knew what to do with women. I wondered what Titty here would look like after I'd had my way with her for a bit. Is that what she wanted to know? Did she even know enough to wonder about that?

I found I rather liked the idea of being handsome, and that this artsy, shabby-chic chickie had told me so.

I shrugged, affecting boredom. "And so?" I had an inkling of what I thought she wanted, but first I wanted to be sure, and second, I wanted her to say it.

She blushed fiercely, but lifted her chin and met my eyes. "I want you to show me what to do with her."

She wanted me to pop her lesbian cherry. Big Blue suddenly seemed very big in my pants. But she didn't want a fucking. She could get that from any guy. No, she wanted to know how to make Janey happy, pinch a clit, lick a tit.

I admit the idea of making out with a baby dyke had appeal. I mean she was cute and I liked her body. But what could I teach her?

I remember my dad telling one of his buddies how his dad took him to a whorehouse so he would know how to make a woman happy. He missed the most important part of making a woman happy, the part where you're family, where you're in it for the love.

Like I knew about that. But, yeah, I could tell her how to please this woman she was chasing.

"Do you know how to make yourself come?" I asked.

"Wha-wha-what?" she stammered.

"Have you ever looked at your pussy in the mirror? Do you know how it works?"

"Yes," she said, looking around to see if anyone had heard. She'd lost the spunk that had brought her to my table.

"Yes, what?" I pressed. "Have you seen your twat, or do you know how your cunt works?"

She flushed, whether from the words or the idea, it didn't matter.

"Well?"

"Not in any great detail," she said softly. "Will you show me?"

She was asking for what amounted to a mercy guided-practice session.

I was a hypocrite, but she thought I was handsome. I nodded. "Okay. I'll show you."

"When?"

"When do you want?"

"Now."

I looked at my coffee and half-eaten éclair. And the paper I'd just started. I could get them to go, but it's kind of like watching *Sunday Morning*. If you don't watch the show Sunday morning, it's just wrong. I would have to let it all go. Just this once.

"Okay. I'm around the corner and down a block." I stood, put my jacket on, and picked up my stuff. The dishes went into the bus tub. The paper went on the tray next to it so someone else could enjoy it.

Opening the door, I gestured her through it. The breeze smelled like spring. The streetlights and neon business signs shone in pools that broke into crazy wavering lines when cars drove through them.

I kept thinking of how hypocritical I was. This baby dyke thought I was taking her to learn to make love. I knew nothing of love. I almost called it off right there.

"I went to a gallery showing of your work two years ago," she said shyly.

"And what did you think?"

"I like your later stuff better than the older stuff."

I wasn't sure if I felt annoyed or pleased. Maybe I should go with pleased. After all, she thought I was handsome.

"Me too."

She didn't say anything else, but I knew she was looking at me out of the corner of her eye as we walked.

I unlocked the front door, glad that I'd left the living room lamp on. And even more pleased that I'd tidied up yesterday. Somehow, I'd hate to have her think I lived like a slob.

Mr. Big Cat eyed us from the corner of the dark-red floral couch that I could never bear to kill. He couldn't decide whether to run at this strange intrusion and stared, his deep-green eyes wide, from her to me, questioning my judgment at bringing a stranger into the house.

I did, too.

The warmth of his current position won out. He put his head back down and watched as Miss Titty laid her bag on the tan wing chair to the left of the door.

I closed the door and she turned to me. "Now what?"

Now what, indeed.

"Come with me."

I led her to my room and turned on the lamps on the bedside tables to give enough light to be useful, but not make things clinical. I was glad again that I'd made the bed.

I wanted her to think highly of me when she saw me in my environment. After all, I told myself, she liked my work, she thought I was handsome.

"Strip," I said, sitting in the nubby mauve overstuffed chair in the corner and putting my feet up on the hassock. I steepled my hands and waited.

"What does this have to do with knowing what to do with a woman?" She put her hands on her hips, arms akimbo. Her face was fierce, her eyes blazing. She was adorable.

"See here, Titty. It's like this. You can't know what to do with a woman until you know what to do with yourself and be comfortable with it. And your answers to my questions in the cafe tell me you aren't. Making love is not groping at each other through a curtain in the dark. It's real and immediate. Looking at each other, asking her what feels good, learning how to give it to her, telling her what you want and how to give it."

Gawd, I sounded like an expert.

"What do you want, Titty? What makes your pussy get wet and squishy?"

She stared at me, the fierceness leaking out of her.

"I think this was not a good idea," she said.

I shook my head. "No, I think you aren't as brave as you thought you were. I think you wanted me to say, 'Touch her here, like this, whisper in her ear.' But if you can't tell me what turns you on, can't look at your own pussy, then all your dreams for this woman are just masturbation fantasies."

She stared at me, her mouth working like she was going to say something snappy, but finally she sighed, pulled her shirt over her head defiantly, and dropped it on the floor.

Maybe I could do this.

Her boots, pants, and underpants followed. They were boy underpants, which made me get more wet and squishy. There's something virginal and innocent about them, and that's exciting, even when it's a lie. Maybe especially when it's a lie.

"Let me look at you."

She struck a pose and looked up at the ceiling.

"Look at me. I'm your lover. You want me to enjoy looking at you. You want to turn me on. You want to be turned on by me looking at you, wanting you."

"Do you want me?"

Her body was slender, yet to acquire the curves it would have in a few years. The bush that crowned her pussy was brown, unlike her hair, and cropped short enough that I could see her lips.

I couldn't count all the ways I wanted her.

"Open the top drawer of the dresser and take out the hand mirror."

She sighed when she realized where I was going, but did as I said.

"Take a gander at yourself. Open up your lips; really check your equipment."

Little Miss Titty lowered the big round mirror, angled it, and used one finger to spread a lip to the side so she could get a look at her quim.

I could smell her—sweat, musk, and some kind of hair product. My pussy twinged and I squirmed so Big Blue pressed against me.

"Now, slip your finger between your lips and give yourself a good jilling."

"I can't, I need lube."

I gestured to the left bedside table. "In the drawer."

She turned and I got a look at her perky bubble ass. Just the kind I like to see laid over my lap. With her fair skin, she would redden up nicely.

But that was not on the menu.

She returned to her position, opened the bottle, poured a bit on her fingers, and went to work. She tried looking at me, but pretty soon she'd forgotten about me, wrapped up in pleasuring herself.

"You look so beautiful working your clit. It makes me want to finger-fuck you." I wanted to do more than that, but this made a nice entry.

"It does?" I saw the jolt of pleasure run down from her brain and into her pussy as she blushed.

"Yeah, but first I want to kiss you. Do you want me to kiss you?"

"Yes."

"Yes, what?"

"Yes, Louden, I want you to kiss me."

"I like it when you say my name." I stood and took her in my arms. Gawd, I'd forgotten what young flesh felt like. I tilted her face up to mine and kissed her. She gave back as good as she got and I pulled her hips against mine. It was electric.

I took her tender breasts in my hands and rolled the tiny nipples in my thumb and forefinger. Then I leaned down to suckle them like I'd wanted to.

Her skin was soft, smooth, new, and I could smell her sweat and the musk rising up between us.

She groaned.

"You like that?"

"I do. Uh, I really like that."

My teeth were grazing her nipples.

"That's good." It turned me on for her to tell me she liked what I was doing. "What do you want me to do?"

"Do?"

"Yes, ask for what you want. I want to pleasure you. So tell me how." This was so novel, very exciting.

"I don't know. What you're doing feels good."

I left off and kissed her. "Do you like this? This?" I took her bottom lip in my teeth and sucked lightly.

"Yes, but kiss me. Kiss me hard."

I obliged and we tongue wrestled. Her arms went around me and I jerked as desire flooded me. Desire and something else. Something I'd forgotten, left behind.

When I reached between her legs, her quim was hot and swollen. I found the doorbell and rang it good, giving her a clue as to what would happen when she opened the door to let me come in.

"Is this right? Am I getting it?"

She moaned and I took her by the back of her hair and pulled her head so I could look her in the eye. "You have to tell me or I'm just guessing," I lied. "Everyone is different, everyone wants it their way. Tell me your way."

"Uh, down, a little more, and circles, make circles," Miss Titty said, her face growing red. That shy admission turned me on. I wanted to see her splayed out on the bed, open to me, but I wanted it on her terms.

I wondered what Karen's terms would be. Oh, we negotiated, but I had discovered her desires and needs while she was cuffed and vulnerable. I never asked her. I learned by reaction.

Miss Titty pulled on my belt and opened my pants, her tiny hands cold as they slid under the waistband and down to my briefs. She boldly slid her hands into them and then paused as she felt Big Blue's harness. I watched her face as she followed the straps down, her eyes confused and then big as she realized what she was touching.

"You have a dildo?"

"I pack, yes, but I'm not going to fuck you."

"You aren't?"

"Do you intend to fuck this woman you want?"

She stared at me for a long moment as she replayed whatever fantasy she had going. "No," she finally said. "No, I never thought of it."

"Well, then, no fucking." I traded my finger for my thumb on the doorbell and then slid a finger in, curled, reaching up high. She humped, opening up so I could have as much as I wanted.

She moaned softly, her eyes shutting in bliss. Her mouth was open and those darling crooked teeth peeked out from under those bow-shaped lips.

I kissed her gently and lifted her up. She was light, like nothing, and, in three steps, I had laid her on the bed. I looked down at her, her legs open, the lube on her snatch shining in the lamplight, her hair tousled, her tits red, the tiny nipples standing as tall as they could.

"Gawd, you are beautiful. I want to make love to you."

I hadn't done that to a woman in years. I had fucked

them, spanked them, flogged them, and we had enjoyed it. Always hard, wicked, nasty, but never tender.

I knelt between her legs.

Kissing her mouth, nibbling my way down her neck, I paused to lick her earlobes, which made her laugh and I smiled.

"Making love should be beautiful and funny," I murmured, remembering how Barbara and I'd had jokes that became private ways to make love in public.

"It should be filled with naughty phrases, filthy words, and jokes that you will cherish, that keep you close even when you're not in bed," I said.

I worked my way down her breasts, nipping and licking, teasing those tiny nipples with my tongue, lightly, never biting. I held her waist, my hands nestled between her hips and ribs, my thumbs arching over her belly button, making it the center of a temple that I worshipped with my tongue.

"Ah, that is weird."

"Good weird or bad weird?"

"It's just weird to have your tongue in my belly button."

"Good to know," I said. "No belly-button fucking."

She laughed and I moved on down to her snatch. I blew gently on it and she groaned.

"Do you like that?"

"Yes, oh, yes," she said.

"What do you want me to do?"

"Whatever you want to do."

"No, because then you're a plaything. And this is making love."

"But I don't know what I want," she wailed.

"Okay then," I slid my finger between her lips and

played the doorbell. "Number one or"—I pulled out and knelt over her to put my tongue between her lips, touching her clit—"Number two."

She leapt like a racehorse from the gate and only my hands on her waist kept her in place.

"Oh, oh, number two. Yes, number two."

Laughing, I went back down on her, "Number one or number two," I said into her snatch as I changed techniques, positions, speed, pressure.

Little by little we discovered what made her come, and come hard she did, with her pelvis smashed to my mouth, three fingers in her twat, and her hands gripping my head to hold me where she wanted me.

Afterward, I crawled up to lie beside her. She was tiny when I cuddled her. I felt protective and warm.

"So that's how women make love," she said, sleepily.

"That's enough to get you going. Ask questions, be curious, be brave."

I felt like a hypocrite, thinking of Karen cuffed to the cross, completely open to whatever I had negotiated with her. It was pleasurable, but always at arm's length. She was beautiful, caring, but I had been too wary of what Barbara had wanted to let myself go anywhere near that with another woman.

"And now it's time for you to get out of here."

She looked up at me. "You don't want me to, uh, practice on you?"

I didn't think I could bear that. And something told me it would be easy for her to lose sight of her objective with her face buried between my legs.

"Nah, go practice with the woman you're chasing. Go on, get up, get out of here."

She rolled out of bed, and went to the bathroom. After she cleaned up, she dressed and followed me to the living room, where she gathered her bag from the chair. I opened the door. She paused, reached up, and kissed me gently. "Thanks, Louden."

I shrugged. "Go get 'em, Titty."

She blushed and play-socked my arm as she left.

I sat on the couch and sighed.

Barbara was a long time ago.

And Karen was a totally different woman.

I pulled my cell phone out and dialed.

"Whattya doin'? Want some company? Yeah, really. No, I'm all right. Great, I'll be there in twenty, no, twenty-five." It would take at least five to run in and grab some flowers at the market. And maybe a bottle of wine. Yeah, I knew she liked wine, although we never drank before we played and she was too out of it afterward.

Maybe it would be interesting to see what would happen closer than arm's length.

MOJAVE

Dena Hankins

My guts rose before the rest of me as I crested the sandy hill. Anything could be on the other side. Brush. Another four-wheeler. A hippy gathering. A twenty-foot drop-off.

The springs of the Odyssey rang as the small vehicle's weight came off its wheels. I launched it off the hill as fast as it would go and almost got some air. The little machine's roll bars and wrist straps and harness formed an exoskeleton of hard steel. I wanted to throw it against the world, knock the world around a bit.

Nothing on the other side except more trail. I could ride for hours in the Mojave around Edwards Air Force Base without seeing another person. Out in bluegrass country, I used to scream. Walk out my front door and push the stillness right out of me through my mouth. I thought it would be better after I left those slow hills and slow trees and slow crops behind.

I'm not military. I teach math to adolescents who hate me, who barely know each other with all the moving they do. Every conversation feels like déjà vu, and every kid thinks they're unique. The odd talented one rarely catches fire with it. The future physicists and engineers are few and far between.

But just behind base housing is the Mojave.

I thought about jerking the wheel as I came up on a scrap of hardy grass the color of sand. Hitting a clump with the side of the wheel would flip the little four-wheeler right over. The wrist straps keep me from automatically putting my hand out and getting it broken. I rotated my wrists against the nylon webbing.

Instead, I set myself at the tallest hill around—a couple hundred feet. Mysterious military antennae sprouted from the top, artificially high, and a rutted dirt track speared straight up a ridge on the side. The little motor whined as I sped at the hill, determined to find a limit somewhere and thinking this could be it. I hit the abrupt incline and was tossed into the sky. I hardly touched the dirt, fat knobby tires slipping in grit. The motor struggled to maintain my momentum, but gravity defied the chugging pistons. I rocked in my harness as though I could swim through the air to the top. On such a steep grade, I might not be able to get back down without burning out the brakes or racing down so fast that I crashed in a truly violent, uncontrolled way.

I shuddered with life.

The Odyssey groaned and the smell of burning dust came from the overheating engine. I urged the machine at the last, steepest portion.

My right front tire came off the edge of the rut and the last of my momentum bounced the front end high enough that gravity switched directions. The wheels kept going, right over my head, and I steered the air in an unthinking attempt at control.

Upside down and beyond, I yelped my abandoned joy. The roll bars took the impact and the Odyssey slid, upside down, about fifty feet downhill. Dust invaded my throat and eyes, silencing and blinding me.

My lips shifted grit across my teeth and gums. My shoulders and chest ached where the harness held me tight to the seat above me. When I opened my painful eyes, my rashed wrists made a red counterpart to my white knuckles.

My head sang, thick and brilliantly red, with adrenaline and gravity-fed blood. I slipped my hands from the straps, reached over my head, and touched the ground with pulsing fingertips. Did I want down or was I exactly where I needed to be, hanging upside down on a man-made mountain in the middle of nowhere? The flashing memory of my futile attempt at control spurred me to laughter, which turned into coughing, which morphed into screams that shook with my shuddering abdomen and tore me open.

"What's wrong? Are you hurt?"

Self-consciousness sprang into being. My voice stopped short. The entire picture came to me clearly. The overturned four-wheeler with a deranged screamer digging into the sand under her head with fiery desperation.

Why did it have to be Phoebe?

I needed to be upright. I needed dignity, faked or real, but for that I needed to get out of the harness.

My fingertips burned from the sand and Phoebe's gentle hand covered mine on the four-way harness buckle. Phoebe teaches English, comp and lit, to the seniors and we had chatted some in the teacher's lounge, though I'd imagined doing more. Her hand on mine sparked a favorite fantasy: driving my hand into her pussy with hard thrusts of my hips, her hands cupping her tits like offerings.

"Come on. We'll get you out, but you have to be ready for the drop."

Right. I took a deep, dry breath. I had no suggestions.

She didn't need any. She arranged herself under me, inside the buried roll bars, with competent economy of action, and ducked her head inside to sit up next to me. If I turned my head, I could kiss her belly. We both smelled sweaty and I wondered what she thought of my scent. Hers made me breathe deep and want to nose at her crotch like a dog.

She caught my upside-down eye and said, "I've got you, Van."

The aftermath of excitement had me shaking a bit. The sky behind her head was pure white and her face, even in the shadow of the Odyssey, looked overexposed. Only the dark, dark brows, the deep red of her lips, and the mink of her black eyes contained enough contrast to coalesce in my blown-out vision.

While I inspected her and tried to stop shivering, she inched me away from the seatback. She pushed an arm behind me as she loosened the shoulder straps and my shoulder pressed into her soft chest.

"Are you ready?"

Before I could squeak, she pushed the pad in the middle of the harness and all four straps fell away.

I dropped, my head and neck guided into her lap. She grunted and I let my legs fall out the side so I wouldn't jackknife right on top of her. My anklebone hit the ground hard, uncontrolled, but her legs cushioned my hip.

Gently, she smoothed my hair back from my face. "Okay?"

"Yeah." I croaked a bit over the word and cleared my throat before trying again. "You okay?"

"I'm fine."

I couldn't find the professional politeness I'd used with her for months, hiding my attraction. "Phoebe, I—"

"Don't talk. You need water."

The words burned my throat more than the dust, but I stopped. I didn't know exactly what I'd been about to say anyway.

Excuses? Explanations?

Why? I was just another nature-lover out looking around, except that I'd turtled my four-wheeler and been found screaming by a coworker I had a crush on.

I scrambled off Phoebe's lap, bumping my shoulder on the roll bar and scooting gracelessly in a semicircle that slid the back of my neck across her thigh.

"Slowly, Vanessa." She gripped my shoulder and slipped out of the roll-bar cage after me. The blood that had pooled in my head ran downhill toward my feet and left me light-headed, so I lay flat on the coarse sand. The bright red sun beat through my eyelids.

"Better." Phoebe's teacher voice grated on my nerves just enough that I wanted to act adult and together, like someone who didn't need commands and comfort. I wasn't sure I was that person, though. I wanted to cry and, whether it was from emotion or adrenaline crash, the heat of her body next to mine made me yearn to hide there.

"Can you move everything? Arms, legs? Neck, shoulders?"

I wiggled obediently as she named body parts and everything worked, though I ached over most of my body.

"Let's get you to my campsite. I have a first-aid kit."

Of course you do, I didn't say.

I tightened my abs—ow—and sat up before opening my eyes. It was the right move, since even the sand between my knees was brighter than I could handle. I blinked until my vision cleared and I could see Phoebe sitting next to me, waiting quietly.

I looked at the Odyssey. If Phoebe and I could roll it over, could we stop it from taking off downhill as soon as the wheels hit the ground? I didn't even feel up to trying.

"Come on, Van. Let's see if you can stand."

I watched her rise and put my hands flat on the hot sand. The incline was enough that standing wouldn't be hard, but she would want to steady me. I wasn't sure I wanted to be touched. I didn't feel like I had any skin.

The sand burned harder on my fingertips and I looked at my hands. My bare wrists looked bad, but my fingertips stole my attention. They throbbed in answer to my questioning look. *Yes, you fucked us up royally*. Each one swelled raw and red, and fine dust sparkled in the tiny drops of blood that welled here and there.

Phoebe reached out and I jerked. She stopped, a questioning look on her face, and then stood. I don't know whether I blushed at giving away . . . something . . . but she put her hand out, fingers up, and spoke quietly. "Give me your hand."

I did, going palm to palm in an arm-wrestling grip that didn't require me to hold on very hard. We pulled together and she put her hand under my elbow as I rose. Her touch unraveled my calm enough to make me lean toward her, but not enough for me to step into her arms for the hug I wanted so badly.

Her hand slid up my arm and squeezed. A flickering question—*did she just feel up my biceps?*—gave way to the realization that she wasn't going to release my hand until I showed I could stand on my own.

I straightened and took a deep breath, which started me coughing again. She let go so I could cover my mouth but stayed close. My head was so clear it felt empty, and I could see for a hundred miles around.

"What the hell?" A carpet of lavender-flecked yellow spread across the sand, greens sparked against the ubiquitous tan, and even the Joshua trees looked like they were having a good stretch.

"The flowers? Amazing, isn't it? I come out here after every rain, if I can." Phoebe scanned the desert and I saw her absorb the short-term vitality of the wetted land. I burst into flower and turned to her, raising my lips for her kiss.

She jolted and her expression flickered between surprise, temptation, and something else, something that made her hesitate and pull away.

I turned and stumbled blindly toward the upside-down four-wheeler.

"Come on, Vanessa. My camp's this way."

She didn't touch me, just stood in my way. How she'd gotten in front of me, I had no idea. Okay. We were going to play it cool, like I'd never tried to kiss her. Like I'd never stomped on her heavenly moment with an unwelcome pass.

The ache in my ankle battled for attention with all the other places I hurt, and I focused on walking carefully up the steep grade to her campsite near the fenced antennae. The last thing I needed was to humiliate myself further by falling.

Phoebe's camp consisted of a small tent, big enough to sit up in and shaded by a fly, and a rock-edged impromptu fire pit. She went to her knees in front of the tent and unzipped it. As much as I wanted to, I couldn't look away from the curve of her waist and thickness of her haunches.

She pulled out a hiking pack. I stood, awkward, and waited for instructions. The first-aid kit was in the front pocket and she tossed it back into the tent, leaving the pack on the dirt. "Let's get out of the sun."

A distinct urge to back away was no match for her magnetism. I'm not one to get in trouble taking stupid dares, but I wanted to be in that tent with her.

She knelt to the side of the entrance, her hands flat on her thighs, for the split second it took to decide I'd do as she said. I creaked down to my hands and knees, keeping my raw fingertips off the sand, and shuffled across the zippered threshold.

A flat pallet of dense foam spanned two-thirds of the tent's width. I shoved aside her sleeping bag so I wouldn't get it dusty, collapsed on my side, and rolled onto my back.

Phoebe appeared over my feet and crawled up next to me. She pushed the first-aid kit ahead of her in a yellowish-green glow diffused by two layers of nylon. I was taking up too much space, though I was the smaller by far, so I scooted to the edge of the tent. The empty span of pallet looked huge until she perched on its edge and folded her legs to one side.

As she rummaged through the first-aid kit, I tried to control my breathing. The heat of our bodies wrestled with the breeze coming in the shaded opening. Sweat pooled in my belly button and steamed in the crease of my thighs.

Without a word, Phoebe took my hand and cleaned the tips of my fingers with antiseptic cloths. The sting helped distract me from her hip next to mine and her thigh under my arm and her strong hand turning mine this way and that. She put my hand down beside my head, palm up and fingers curled, as though arranging me for a cheesecake photo, then took my other hand and pulled it across my body.

The angle of her shoulders and the curve of her back soaked into me. Leaning across me, one side of her waist formed rolls and the other stretched smooth. I wondered if she could smell my pussy.

She released my hand and stroked my collarbone. Hope and fear froze me.

"Your harness really messed you up. Let me put arnica on the bruises." Her gaze flickered up to meet mine, then she looked back at the strap marks.

"I don't . . . " Her eyes followed her fingers as they stroked my bruised skin and the shadow pain was nothing to the pleasure. "Phoebe, I can't be calm with your hands on me."

"Are you really after calm, Vanessa? You seem to be running pretty hard from calm." She slid her hand over my throat and down my other shoulder. My tits ached and maybe I arched toward her. Phoebe surveyed the low topography of my chest, my nipples too hard. "Wouldn't you prefer excitement?" She put both hands flat on my tits and pressed them against my ribs.

"Don't fuck with me, Phoebe." I screwed my eyes closed and balled my sore fingers into fists.

"Shhh. This isn't a tease, Van. You're so tightly wound. Has it been a long time?"

"I get myself off just fine." She never stopped touching my tits, but her grip changed to a slow pull and roll of my nipples through the ribbed cotton of my tee. I never had an inkling of how a person could come like that until Phoebe did it.

Her laugh was low, indulgent. "I bet you orgasm fast and fall asleep slow."

I opened my eyes. How did she know?

"I'm going to touch you everywhere and take my time. I'll get to know what you like, but I'll give it to you on my schedule. Are you ready for this?"

Was there any other answer? "Yes."

"That's what you think." Phoebe stripped my shirt off over my head, cotton wet with sweat. She squeezed a dollop of cream into her palm and recapped the tube. "Arnica." With broad strokes, she spread the cream over my shoulders, between my tits, and along my ribs in the shape of the Odyssey's harness.

The ache of pressure on fresh bruises tasted like metal and made me aware of the layers of my flesh. She moved skin over muscle and bone, rubbing the cream into me. The massage continued down my arms, one at a time, and up my neck. Without hesitation, she unsnapped my shorts and tugged them off.

A freshet of breeze circled the tent and my muscles clenched and released. I imagined her mouth on my pussy, her hands rubbing my clit, her knuckles rubbing inside me.

She massaged my legs, slowly and firmly moving my limbs, stretching and pressing and rubbing. When her hands spanned my hips and massaged the tight tendons on each side of my pubic bone, I let her take the tension and anxiety. My legs lolled on the pallet and she knelt between them. I closed my eyes.

Without a change in her manner, she worked her fingers deep into the muscles around my pussy. Her knuckles dug in without opening me up. Muscles I never thought about stretched under her fingers. The edges of her hands woke my clit without touching its tip and I remembered a diagram I'd seen about the clit's wishbone shape, how it extends inside past the vagina.

Phoebe rubbed my labia, pinched and pulled them. I looked up at her. Was this the signal? Were we going to start fucking? But she alternated her touch, deep massage, pulling, pushing, rubbing, nothing that felt to me like the flurry and hubbub of sex. I was heavy and hot and unraveling bit by bit, but I had no idea where it was heading. My tongue arched for the press of her nipples and my hands reached for her but fell short.

"You're so wet. Just pouring with sweat and pussy juice."

I hummed in response, though she didn't seem to need any. The hum felt good, though, vibrating low like her touch. When she pressed deep, I hummed again and she nodded. "That's right. Feels good." The abstraction in her voice and the intense concentration of her hands pushed me to arch and circle. The ever-smaller part of me observing had nothing to say about it. It didn't matter if it was sexy, if it looked good. It felt amazing.

Phoebe spread my labia wide and massaged their wet inner surfaces, stroking path after path before her fingers dipped inside me and kept stroking. She traced ovals with long sides, still with the pressure and pacing of her massage. Flooded and overflowing, I realized that this was sex, that we'd been fucking the whole time.

I reached for my clit and flinched at the stinging salt juice on my abraded fingertips.

"Don't. You don't have to chase this. This come isn't a wild bronc you need to break. It's a skittish horse, full of heart, and you need to let it come to you."

I didn't know what she meant, but I let my hand fall away. Heavy, full of pressure and slow friction, Phoebe surged against me like tidal waves. She filled my pussy and touched every part of my clit at the same time. She ground into me and withdrew and I groaned low.

Heavier, she pushed in and I pushed back. We rode the same wave and my gasps and groans resonated in the air between us. Instead of a click and tumble, I built and built, so far past orgasm that I realized I must have been coming forever.

I stared into Phoebe's fierce eyes, her lips drawn back in triumph. That thing I chased into the desert, chased from my lungs, and hunted all my life. She tapped that well and it poured from me in an abundance I'd never imagined.

I don't know how long we rode those waves, but for the first time in my life, I came slow and fell asleep fast.

Several hours later, I woke to watch the sun set over the brilliant, living desert with Phoebe. Then I showed her that, though I was a teacher by trade, I was an even better learner.

SUPER

Heather Day

The amazing thing is, I met her in a comic shop. Not one of the big ones down in London either; that wouldn't have been so incredible. No, it was just the local dive, the one smelling of old books, with torn Vampirella posters on the walls and a sun-bleached, cardboard cutout of R2-D2 in the window.

It was a Saturday afternoon and, as per my usual routine, I'd rolled up at Comicool to collect my weekly stash, check out any new titles that had arrived, and flirt with Josh, the geek behind the counter who worked on his own comic in between serving customers. But today, something stopped me in my tracks. The shop was normally busy on a Saturday, but it was usually full of excitable children and gangs of dorky teenage boys. There was not normally a superhot chick in stripy, knee-high socks and a combat dress perusing the indie comics section. I caught my breath and steadied my nerves.

Trying to play it cool, I waved hi to Josh and idled over

to the superhero section. This was purely to get a better look at her, you understand; I would not be caught dead reading that stuff.

Peering furtively at her, I noticed that she had already chosen a thick pile of books and comics and was now trying to balance them on her left hand while taking another off the shelf with her right. I tried to squint at her choices and from what I could see it looked like she had good taste. And she was definitely hot; tall and slender and rocking the geek look. I guessed that she was several years older than me. She wore thick-rimmed glasses, had several ear piercings, and her hair was tied in ironic bunches. It was mostly black with a few green streaks. I should start a conversation with her, I decided. After all, how often does this kind of chance, or this kind of girl, come along? Okay so there was no way she'd actually be interested in someone as dorky as me, but I'd had so much experience of rejection, surely I was immune to it by now . . . .

Thankfully, my obsessive procrastination was stopped in its tracks by the work of gravity. The object of my adoration placed another comic on top of her already wobbly pile and that was enough to cause a landslide effect. Enraptured with her as I was, I noticed this before she did and leapt across the shop in order to save the plunging books. As I did so I dropped to a crouch, which put me in the embarrassing position of having to look up at her as she first noticed me, as if I'd just proposed to her or was trying to look up her dress.

"Wow, thanks! How heroic."

I was too busy enjoying our new proximity to worry about whether or not she was being sarcastic. Up close I could see a light sprinkling of freckles across her face, and that there was a little green mixed in with the brown of her eyes.

"No problem, it's my sworn duty to protect comic books everywhere."

"That's cute."

"Heh, yeah." I straightened up and handed back her comics, preparing to continue my poor attempt at flirting when I realized with horror what book lay on the top of her pile. The telltale primary colors and bulging muscles made my eyes hurt.

"Oh . . . you like superheroes?"

"Hell yes, doesn't everyone?"

"Erm, yeah, they're great," I lied. Out of the corner of my eye, I saw Josh raise an eyebrow at me.

"I've got all the classics," she went on, "and I love the new ways artists are experimenting with the genre."

Our match rating was going down before my very eyes. How could fate be so cruel, to send me such a beauty only to reveal her as a superhero fan? And yet, I found that this unfortunate fact didn't stop me from imagining what it would feel like to have her legs wrapped around me, her mouth on mine . . . .

"Oh yes," I said, "I totally agree."

"Cool," she said, before going to pay for her comics. Once she was done and on her way out the door she turned round to look at me. I pretended to be absorbed in a display of horror movie memorabilia in order to disguise the fact that I'd been staring at her the whole time. I don't think the ploy worked.

"Bye," she laughed.

I blushed and waved.

"Wow," I said, turning to Josh once she was outside, "I

think I'm in love. Did you see her? The hair? The glasses?"

"The love of superhero comics."

Josh looked at me pointedly as he handed me my comic stash. We've had many discussions over the years about the relative merits of different comic genres and he knows full well how I feel about superheroes. He knows that when it comes to comics, I want complex, layered stories and avant-garde artwork. What I don't want is improbably proportioned people in spandex spouting morality at me.

"I know, I know, you think I'm a snob," I retorted, "but I can't help how I feel. Do you think there could ever be a future for me and her?"

"The way you two looked at each other? I'm sure a little thing like that wouldn't get in your way."

As I handed over most of the money in my purse, Josh did a quick drawing and slid it across the counter to me. It was a cartoon version of me and my new crush, locked in a passionate snog, my hands on her perky boobs.

"Josh," I said, "you are such a pervert."

As he rang up the sale on the till, I folded up the drawing and slipped it discreetly into my pocket.

"You're welcome," he said, not looking up.

I laughed as he handed me my change.

"See you, Josh."

"See you, supergirl."

I had a quick check to see if there were any kids around before flipping him the finger as I left.

I couldn't get her off my mind for the rest of the week. Her pouty lips and lengthy legs haunted me as I slept, as I read, as I got ready for work and mooched around the office. I thought again and again how amazing it was that we'd even met, that we'd been in the same shop at the same time. Fate must have had something to do with it, surely?

After all, I was planning on that trip being my last to the comic shop for a while. Much as I loved the place and needed my weekly comic fix, the simple truth was that I was broke. In my final year of university, the economy had decided to take a nosedive and I ended up graduating at the most inopportune time in decades. As I entered a ridiculously competitive marketplace, suddenly my degree in graphic design looked comical. When my friends with firsts in business and management couldn't get jobs, I knew I had little hope of landing anything within the creative industries.

After lots of depressing rejections, I managed to get an admin position at a marketing consultancy. So far it had been a fun round of tea-making, filing, and photocopying, but at least I was in the right industry and, most importantly, earning my own money. With a bit of luck and a lot of discipline, it wouldn't be long until I'd saved up enough to finally move out of my parents' house and into a place of my own.

That, though, was going to mean sacrifices. Sprawled on my bed later that week, I tried to imagine what I would do for entertainment when I didn't have my regular supply of comics coming in. It was a depressing thought. Maybe I should go back to drawing my own, I thought idly, something I hadn't done for years.

Then I remembered Josh's pervy drawing and went to fetch it from my bedside drawer. I'd been taking sneaky peeks at it all week. Josh can be an idiot, but he's a good artist and he'd captured something about her, even in that quick sketch.

Saturday was approaching once again and I'd already decided to go back to the shop on the off chance she'd return. I really couldn't afford to buy anything, but maybe I could just hang around looking cool and impress her with my sharp banter and encyclopaedic comic-book knowledge. I wondered whether she was the type who liked to dress up, donning tight-fitting leotards, capes, and eye masks to add an extra edge in the bedroom. Maybe I could play the evil villain, tie her up, and have my wicked way with her . . . *Hm,* I thought, *maybe this could work out after all.*

Once conjured, the X-rated visuals in my head wouldn't leave, so I had no choice but to lock the door and wriggle my hand down under my jeans. As I moved it in tiny circles, the pace of my fantasies increased and soon my clit was soaking. I pictured stripping her down to bare flesh, all perky boobs and glistening pussy.

I got as far as imagining crouching down before her to suck her all the way to orgasm, before shuddering my way through an incredibly powerful climax of my own.

Oh god, I thought as I gradually came down from the high, *I am so in trouble.*

The following Saturday I got to the shop at an indecently early hour and needless to say, she was not yet there. I wasted an hour trawling through back issues of comics I'd never heard of, trying to avoid the temptation to buy something, and chatting idly to Josh.

Suddenly the bell above the door announced someone entering the shop. Josh and I both turned to stare at the newcomer. My heart started beating wildly; it was her.

"Hello again." She waved at me.

"Hi!" I managed. She looked even better than last week; this time rocking a tight, strappy top showing a sexy anime character and baggy jeans held up with a studded belt. Her black-and-green hair was loose, just reaching to her shoulders, and she assessed me from behind those same hot-as-fuck glasses.

"I love your top," I said.

"Thanks," she replied. "Oh, I brought something to show you."

She walked over to the battered sofas kept at the back of the shop and I followed. She flopped into the corner of a couch and rummaged in her bag.

"Here you go."

She handed me a rather well-loved copy of a fat little paperback book. The words *Superheroes through the Ages* were spelled out in bold, colorful letters on the front. I groaned inwardly; could I really let this facade go on much longer?

"Oh . . . cool . . . " I said, flipping through it casually and trying to feign interest. "I'll have a proper look later." I placed the offending book on the arm of the sofa. "So, how's your week been?"

"Exhausting." She flopped farther back on the sofa to emphasize her point. "I have a full-time job, but I've got this great idea for a comic that I've been working on in the evenings. The only trouble is, I stay up too late working on it. My coffee consumption's through the roof."

"Oh, you draw?"

"God no, I can't even do stick men. I write. I'll need to find an artist, if this idea ever gets off the ground. Know anyone good?"

"Josh over there's a great artist. And, well, I've dabbled a bit, too."

"Really?" her eyes lit up. "That's so cool! I'd love to see your art. I bet we could create something amazing together."

She was holding me in her steady gaze and I felt excitement coming off her in waves. I was suddenly aware of just how close we were on the sofa, how easy it would be to lean across and kiss her lips, to take her reclining body in my arms . . .

But then the doubts came creeping in.

"I'm not that good, really," I said.

"I bet you are, can I take a look at your work?"

"Maybe if you tell me some of your ideas, I could come up with some character sketches. Don't feel like you have to use them, though."

"You need to have more confidence in your work, um—sorry, what was your name?"

"Janice."

"I'm Beth. You need to have more confidence in your work, Janice. I bet I'll love it."

She squeezed my shoulder in encouragement, causing my nerves to fire into life. We locked eyes for a beat.

"So what's the story about?"

"In a nutshell? Dyke superhero."

"Wow."

"I just think we need more queers in comics, especially superheroes. Naturally, my heroine has a dual personality— shy, bookish girl by day, sexy crime fighter by night. And of course, women everywhere can't help but fall for her."

My imagination was already working overtime. I told her I'd give it a go.

"Great. Well, I better get going, but let's meet here this time next week. Bring some drawings and I can take you back to my flat to go through them, it's only down the road."

"Okay, sounds like a plan. But I'm a bit rusty, you have been warned!"

"Janice," she said, turning to look me square in the face, "I bet you're amazing."

Slowly, she stroked a stray hair that had fallen across my cheek, and tucked it back behind my ear. For a moment I thought she was going to kiss me. Instead she jumped up, blew me a kiss, and was off out the door, a whirlwind of colorful geekiness, leaving me wanting and waiting.

As I walked into the comic shop the following Saturday, with a sketchpad under my arm and freshly-colored hair, my heart started to beat in a way that I had not experienced for quite some time. Then it positively leapt into my mouth when I saw that this week, she had arrived before me.

"Janice, hi!" She was at the till, paying for her comics and waving at me. I waved back awkwardly, desperately trying not to drop my sketchpad. She finished paying and then jogged over to me.

"Right, ready to go?"

"Sure," I said, not actually feeling ready at all, but suddenly rather sick. It had been a very long time since I'd been alone with a girl I liked. As we walked she grabbed my hand to lead the way and talked nonstop about comics. I was starting to think I'd found someone who was even more obsessed than me and how lucky I was, just as her chatter turned inevitably to the one thing I can't stand.

"There's just something about them, you know? The strength, the secret identities, the timeless fight of good against evil. How could anyone not love superheroes?"

"Beats me," I shrugged, hoping to come across as authentically baffled. I couldn't bring myself to expand on my deceit.

Luckily, she saved me from further moral shame by announcing that the small but pleasant-looking block of flats in front of us was where she lived.

"Step into my abode," she said with a flourish.

I felt nervous as I first stepped inside, but quickly began to feel at home. It was comfortably messy and filled with personality; anime girl statues stared down at me from bookshelves and there were several framed, vintage comic covers on the wall. The many bookcases were positively groaning with colorful trade paperbacks and stacks of single issues encased lovingly in protective bags.

"A little over the top, I know." Beth laughed. "But when you've got your own place, you may as well make the most of it."

"I am so jealous."

"You wouldn't be jealous of the bills, though. Anyway." Beth dragged a large coffee table in front of the sofa and cleared it of assorted paperwork and chocolate wrappers. "Let's get down to business."

I placed my sketchpad on the table and settled myself on the sofa, wondering what Beth would make of what she was about to see.

"So I thought about what you said, about your main character being irresistible, and I sort of went from there, really."

She looked at me inquisitively before flipping to the

first page of the pad. Then her expression changed to a mix of surprise and amusement.

"You certainly did, didn't you?"

I had spent the last week perfecting drawings of females in various stages of undress and engaged in various stages of fucking.

"I started off by trying to visualize your main character"—I gestured to the first few drawings, showing a lithe woman with impressive breasts in a cape with her hands on her hips, hair blowing in the wind—"then I thought it was important to get to grips with anatomy, if she's going to be doing a lot of seducing."

I let Beth flip through the rest of the pad, the drawings getting progressively raunchier as she went along.

"Well, Janice," she finally said as she flipped over the last page, "these are quite something. Either you have a magnificent imagination or are a formidably experienced lover."

"Perhaps a little of both." I smirked.

"Care to put that to the test?"

I didn't have time to think of a witty response before she launched herself at me, pinning me back in the sofa and pressing her mouth to mine. She was wild and earnest, massaging my breasts through my top as our tongues danced.

My body met hers with equal ferocity as the weeks of pent-up lust finally found a release. I hooked my fingers inside her waistband and gasped a little as she tweaked my nipples cruelly.

"I've been wanting to do this since I first saw you," she said.

"Oh god, me too."

Talking became obsolete as we delighted in finding more and more ways that our bodies could fit together: breast to breast, arm to waist, mouth to stomach, ever flowing and all with a frantic urgency.

"As much as I want to make this last all day," she whispered between nibbles of my earlobe, "I just don't think I can wait."

In a flash her top was off and hurled to the floor, swiftly followed by her bra. She went to take off the glasses but I stopped her.

"You can leave those on." I smiled.

Her breasts looked pert and delicious but she wouldn't let me get hold of them until she'd got me topless, too.

"Janice, you are so fucking hot."

She traced a line of wet kisses from my mouth, down my neck to my nipples, which she then set about grazing with her teeth and lips.

"Oh . . . fuck . . . " I couldn't manage anything more coherent and my groans grew louder as she unzipped my jeans and found my slick pussy. Her hand strummed my swollen clit, her tongue flicked at my nipple like a woman possessed, and my body was unable to resist.

The orgasm came quickly and overpowered me completely. My whole body flooded with warmth and after the sharp peak of ecstasy, I was left with a divine afterglow.

"That was delicious." I kissed Beth and tugged on her lower lip with my teeth, maneuvering her so that she lay beneath me. "Now it's your turn."

My postorgasm movements were slow and languid and I delighted in the way she writhed and kicked her legs to hurry me along as I peeled her jeans off. I now had this beautiful woman completely naked beneath me and it didn't take long for my body to follow its natural instinct and give her just as much pleasure as she'd given me. My thumbs found her nipples and my mouth latched on to her sweet clit.

"Yes! Oh yes, don't stop. Oh!" Beth grabbed my head, making me giggle and smear her juices all round my mouth. As her moans grew louder, I duly moved my tongue faster across her clit until I could tell she was reaching the point of no return, when I switched to sucking on her wildly.

"Oh fuck!" She grabbed a handful of my hair as she came, which was painful, but in a good way.

As she settled back down to earth, she pulled me down into a sweaty hug.

"Come here," she said, and mashed her lips onto mine so that her juices mingled between us. "That was so yummy. I think I'd like to keep you, if that's okay."

It was more than okay. I couldn't think of anything better, in fact. There was just one tiny confession I had to make first.

"Beth, I really have to tell you something."

"Bloody hell, don't tell me you have a girlfriend?"

"Worse, I'm afraid. I . . . fucking hate superheroes."

"Oh, that? Yeah, I know."

"What?"

"Sweetheart, you left my superhero book at Comicool after I lent it to you last week. Josh handed it back to me this morning." She laughed at my incredulous expression. "I can smell a superhero fan a mile off and honey, you are not one of us."

"Thank god for that." I smiled. "I was so worried about telling you!"

"Oh Janice," she sighed, pulling my face back toward hers, "there was no need to worry; you're all the super I need."

SILENT PASSION

Rose de Fer

Terry closed her eyes, listening to the rattle of film through the projector as the credits scrolled by in their iconic jagged font. It almost seemed a shame to play the soundtrack, as the nostalgic noise was evocative by itself. But she liked this new score, a strange, unearthly blend of music and sound design, all trippy synth and theremin. It suited the dreamy world of *Caligari* perfectly.

It was the first silent movie she had ever seen. She'd been too young to read the translated intertitles, so her dad had told the story for her in a dramatic German accent that made her laugh, but which was also kind of scary.

The wicked Dr. Caligari was more frightening than Cesare, the poor Somnambulist who was forced to kill at his master's command. But it wasn't either of the main characters who haunted her dreams that night. It was Jane, the beautiful girl beloved by two men, Francis and Alan. There was something so otherworldly about her.

Terry had been captivated from her very first appearance.

In the opening scene, Francis was sitting on a park bench with an old man who was telling a mournful tale of being haunted. Then Jane wandered into the frame, her eyes wide with wonder as she gazed at something only she could see.

SPIRITS SURROUND US ON EVERY SIDE.

But Francis wasn't listening to the old man. He was staring at the girl as she drifted past him in a filmy white dress, as though she might be a ghost. Terry identified with Francis instantly. In that moment, she had fallen in love. With Jane, with the movie, with the entire exotic world of silent cinema.

There was no other name she would have chosen when, thirty years later, she finally realized her dream of owning her own vintage cinema. The Caligari had been a true labor of love, a reclamation project that had taken her the better part of two years to renovate and restore to its former glory. But it had been worth it. Now the small Art Deco theater, originally the City Lights Picture Palace, belonged to Terry and was the only dedicated silent film theater in the state.

If only the general public could appreciate what a gem it was.

It was with dismay that she heard people chattering excitedly about the latest blockbusters showing over at the multiplex even while buying tickets to see the classics of a bygone age at the Caligari. They were more dazzled by special effects, 3D, and surround sound than the simplicity of what to them was an ancient, outdated art form, something cheesy and trite. Sure, they laughed at the antics of Charlie Chaplin and Buster Keaton and Harold Lloyd, but they had no real appreciation for the elaborate orchestration behind such stunts.

Even worse was the inappropriate laughter at things just because they were dated. Although, in fairness, that wasn't unique to her audiences; anything older than about ten years seemed a target for ridicule. It was annoying to hear people guffawing over the sight of a rotary dial telephone or a bouncy old jalopy, and more annoying still to see them making fun of the theatrical style of acting of the period. Why couldn't they appreciate these movies for what they were—precious glimpses into the past? Someday their state-of-the-art smartphone might be just as laughable to a future society that had colonized Mars.

And what was up with vampires? Once upon a time they had been monsters. Now they were all moody, broody teens. Terry preferred them when they were scary. And was there ever a scarier vampire than Max Schreck in *Nosferatu*?

More than anything, Terry resented being made to feel old. She wasn't even forty yet, but her inner voice was capable of making her sound like some bitter old lady, yelling at kids to get off her damn lawn.

With a laugh at herself, she shook her head and went to the window in the booth to peer down into the auditorium. Caligari was exhorting Cesare to awaken from his dark night, to tell the fortunes of the people who had come to see him.

She watched the iconic moment as Cesare slowly opened his eyes, staring straight into the lens, into the eyes of everyone watching him. Oh, how that had scared her as a child! What must it have been like for a 1920s audience?

Francis's friend Alan chose a grim question to ask:

HOW LONG WILL I LIVE?

The weird spiky font of the intertitles rendered Cesare's response even more ominous.

TILL DAWN.

The moment had always given her a pleasing little frisson of fear.

Terry looked down into the stalls. It was a slow day. A *very* slow day. But at least her one reliable customer had come. Her *favorite* customer. Terry had never screwed up the courage to approach her, only gazed from afar like some pining lover in a silent melodrama. Like Francis in the opening scene.

The girl was around Terry's age, and she clearly had a fascination for the period. Her black hair was cut in a flapper's chic bob and her slim, boyish figure would have looked perfect in a fringed dress. Or better still—in nothing at all. She could be the reincarnation of Louise Brooks, and Terry had secretly named her "Lulu."

She'd first seen Lulu at a screening of Brooks's most famous film, *Pandora's Box*. That day the girl had been wearing red. Red dress, red cloche hat, red lipstick, and a string of pearls. Terry could hardly believe her eyes. She was like a vision straight from her wildest dreams. And she'd taken center stage in Terry's fantasies ever since.

That night Terry had imagined her wearing nothing but the cloche hat and pearls. Lulu had teased and danced and flirted before finally splaying herself on the bed, open and offering.

Terry's fingers tingled as she lost herself in the fantasy once more, imagining how it would feel to stroke the girl's velvety skin, to kiss her rosebud lips, to press her own breasts against Lulu's. The warm softness of their bodies was intoxicating, belying the fierce urgency of Terry's movements as she ground her hips against her lover's.

Terry slipped the rope of pearls over Lulu's slender neck and teased her naked body with them, drawing them along her spread limbs, over her taut belly, and finally, down between her legs.

Lulu pressed her thighs together, trapping the pearls there. Her eyes blazed with passion as she writhed on the bed, a silent show just for Terry. Then she gasped and cried out, clutching the bedposts as Terry thrust her hand between Lulu's legs, parting them and plunging her fingers deep inside her hot, wet sex. The pearls were next.

Slowly and gently, Terry pushed the smooth beads inside her, two by two. Lulu bit her lip, moaning in ecstasy. Terry stirred the pearls inside her, swirling her finger against them. The sensation was exquisite. At last, she looped her finger around the strand of pearls and drew them out with excruciating deliberation. Lulu tossed her head from side to side, wordlessly begging her for more.

A sudden discordant note on the soundtrack jolted Terry from her fantasy before it could reach its conclusion. She shook her head, remembering where she was. Her face burned and she smiled to herself as she looked down into the stalls for Lulu.

But the auditorium was completely empty. Strange. Terry was sure she'd seen her come in. Perhaps she'd just gone to the restroom. She'd be back in time for the most famous scene, where Cesare is too smitten by Jane to kill her and kidnaps her instead, carrying her through the expressionist wonderland of zigzagging streets and twisted buildings.

Terry indulged herself in a little more of the fantasy,

gently rubbing her fingers together as she imagined the sensation of withdrawing the pearls, their hot sticky wetness. They would taste of Lulu, salty and warm.

She must have zoned out completely because the next time she looked, Cesare was sleepwalking through the town toward Jane's house. Lulu was still nowhere to be seen. Terry's heart sank.

Then a figure emerged from the right side of the screen, just in front of it.

The Somnambulist crept along, feeling his way with his right arm raised high and pressed against the wall, as though listening to a voice inside it only he could hear. And as he did, the figure did the same. Terry's breath caught in her throat. It was *her*. And Terry's eyes went wide as she realized that Lulu was completely naked.

The film played over the canvas of the girl's bare skin, clothing her in light. Her movements were catlike and graceful as she crept along, mirroring the Somnambulist's languid pace. When Cesare reached the edge of the wall and turned the corner, Lulu turned as well, facing into the screen. She could go no farther. The image was distorted across the slender lines of her body, the eerie blue light picking out and highlighting her exquisite shape.

She stopped there, in perfect position for the next scene. Jane's sleeping face shone across the girl's back as Cesare crept slowly toward her, toward them both, from across the room. The suspenseful moment intensified the heat that was spreading through Terry's body. Her sex was pulsing along with the otherworldly music. She was transfixed, frozen to the spot. She could only watch, helpless, as Cesare raised the knife and leaned down toward the sleeping Jane, the naked Lulu.

Then Cesare froze, every bit as transfixed as Terry was. The moment stretched, the music on the soundtrack vibrating as he stared at Jane, unable to follow his master's evil command. He dropped the knife and reached out for her instead. Slowly. So agonizingly slowly.

But when he touched her, she screamed and struggled and at last Terry shook off her paralysis. She left the stuffy little booth and hurried down the stairs to the auditorium, half fearing that Lulu would be gone, carried off by Cesare.

But he was only carrying Jane, dragging her up the sharply angled street. Lulu stood safely below. Waiting.

Terry approached slowly, as Cesare had done. As she drew near she could see the playful smile on the other girl's face. Terry opened her mouth to speak, but the words wouldn't come. She imagined an intertitle conveying her words instead.

YOU'RE SO BEAUTIFUL.

Lulu dipped her head as though she had heard Terry's thought. Then she moved toward her, arms outstretched. For a moment Terry thought she meant to hug her, but Lulu's fingers went straight to the buttons of Terry's shirt instead. Slowly the girl undressed her while Terry stood still, obeying the silent instruction not to move.

Once the cool air kissed her bare flesh, however, her hands fluttered self-consciously to her breasts. She glanced around, but they were quite alone. Lulu peered at her, eyes gleaming in the darkened auditorium. The blue-tinted scene behind them gave her the appearance of a ghost.

But it was certainly no ghost who gently peeled Terry's hands away from covering herself. Lulu's teeth pressed against her full underlip as her eyes roamed over Terry's naked body.

Terry felt herself blush to the roots of her hair and she closed her eyes, surrendering to the girl's scrutiny. Lulu chose the moment of darkness to kiss her. Terry's eyes flew open and then closed again as she relaxed into the kiss. The auditorium smelled of fresh popcorn and Lulu was as warm and soft as butter. She could hardly believe this wasn't all a dream.

She put her hands on Terry's shoulders and gently began backing her toward the front row of seats. She pushed her down and Terry eased herself gratefully into the soft red velvet. Lulu stood before her for a moment before sinking to her knees. Her smile was intoxicating, impish and full of mischief.

Her hands gently cupped Terry's breasts and Terry gasped at the contact. It had been a long time since anyone had touched her like that. She clutched the arms of the seat as Lulu toyed with her stiffening nipples, pinching and finally kissing them. She licked them as if they were candy.

When she pulled back, Terry gave a little whimper of protest. But Lulu wasn't finished. Her hands trailed over Terry's body, down to her thighs. Then her face disappeared as she lowered her head, parting Terry's knees.

The short-cropped hair tickled as Lulu kissed her way up Terry's inner thigh. Terry shuddered with pleasure and held her legs as far apart as the seat would allow. After a moment she felt the warm wetness of Lulu's tongue against her sex and couldn't restrain a little cry. Above them, the film continued, but the images were like clouds, wispy manifestations of their passion. Terry was drowning in ecstasy. If this was a dream, she didn't ever want to wake up.

Lulu moved her tongue in little circling motions around Terry's clit, then sucked the hard little bud into her mouth. The effect was devastating. It was almost too much to take. Terry gasped and clutched at Lulu's hair, urging her on. Her whole body tingled and she writhed against the plush velvet, lost in the sensations.

When the climax came she finally broke the silence, loosing a wild cry into the empty auditorium. Their only audience was the characters on the screen, people from the distant past, frozen in another time and place. They might as well be ghosts.

Terry clung to Lulu as the orgasm sent shock waves through her body, finally fading to pleasant little pulses. A hot blush burned her cheeks and she closed her eyes, burying her face in the silky hair of her mysterious companion.

When Terry finally raised her head, Lulu was smiling at her. Terry opened her mouth to speak, but Lulu placed a finger on her lips. She glanced up at the screen.

YOU MUST BECOME CALIGARI!

The man who had sought to emulate the evil Dr. Caligari was roaming the wild streets, lost in delusions of grand madness, his mind spiraling out of control as the words chased him, floating in the air above him. Terry smiled, relating to the moment. Lulu was a sweet insanity she could surrender to forever. Together they watched the rest of the film, sitting naked in the front row, neither saying a word.

The framing story concluded with Francis in the asylum, all the dreamy weirdness revealed as hallucination.

Dr. Caligari was the director of the asylum. Cesare was mute and harmless. And the beautiful Jane sat on a throne in the center of the room, wearing a crown and believing herself to be a queen. Francis professed his love for her, but she turned her head away, gazing sadly into the distance.

WE QUEENS ARE NOT FREE TO ANSWER THE CALL OF OUR HEART.

As always, the moment gave Terry a little pang of sorrow. Would she wake from this moment to find it had all been a dream, Lulu nothing more than a fantasy, something conjured by her lonely, horny mind to give her pleasure for a moment?

But there was movement beside her. Lulu reached out and held Terry's chin in her hand, turning her face toward her.

"But *we* are free," Lulu said, her voice like music, teasing and soft. "And my heart calls to yours."

Terry jumped, startled by the broken silence. For a moment she couldn't speak, could only stare into Lulu's beautiful eyes, drinking in the sight of her playful grin. She blushed and lowered her head, her arms drifting to cover her nakedness.

Onscreen, the movie was coming to an end.

"Um," Terry said.

Lulu grinned and slowly undulated her fingers in front of Terry's face, imitating Caligari. "Awaken from your dark night . . . "

Terry laughed softly. "Oh, I'm awake," she said. "I don't think I've ever been more awake. But . . . um, have to . . . " She pointed at the screen.

Lulu nodded, still smiling. "I've always wanted to see

the projectionist booth. It's where the magic happens, after all."

Terry smiled, thrilled beyond measure at the thought of taking Lulu into her own little cabinet upstairs. "I'd love to show you," she said. Then, feeling a little bolder, she added, "You're wrong about one thing, though." She reached over, running her fingers over Lulu's breasts. "That's not where the magic happens."

BICYCLING PUTS THE FUN BETWEEN YOUR LEGS

Janelle Reston

"All the nerve endings in my crotch are officially dead," Morgan said when we rolled into the pit stop in New Jersey's Pine Barrens. Our cleats sank into the sandy soil as we dismounted our bicycles and propped them against the closest empty tree trunk. We were about halfway through our eighty-mile route from Philadelphia to the Atlantic shore, and the stop was already teeming with other cyclists taking a break.

In contrast to Morgan's, my crotch wasn't numb at all. It flushed practically every time I looked at her. My nerves down there felt as alive as ever, thank you very much.

I rubbed my palm over her bike saddle, still warm from her body. I felt slightly jealous that it got to spend so much time between her legs. "This seat isn't helping? You loved it at the shop." I'd gone with her the previous week to help her pick it out. Morgan was fairly new to long-distance cycling and had complained about her previous saddle incessantly rubbing against her labia, and not in the good way. This new one was like mine, with a cutout to spare the delicate lady parts.

"It's not my labia that hurt. It's everything else." She pulled her empty water bottle from its cage and walked over to the drink tent a few paces away to cram it full of ice.

Then, in full view of anyone who cared to look, she shoved the bottle down the front of her bike shorts, wriggled her hips to settle it between her thighs, and gave a little shiver of pleasure. "That's much better."

"Ice on your snatch? That's hard-core." I laughed even as a quiver traveled through my own hips. What I wouldn't have given to be that bottle.

"I told you it hurt. I feel like someone put a sledgehammer to my pussy, and not in a good way."

I was too hot from the pedaling to blush, but I ducked my head anyway as I filled my own bottles with Gatorade. "We should check the height and angle of your saddle then. A well-adjusted bike seat shouldn't make you feel like that."

She eyed me. "So your crotch is doing fine?"

"Never been better," I answered, still not looking at her. I was afraid the double meaning would be evident in my eyes, and I wasn't sure I was ready for her to know how I felt about her—not until I could suss out her feelings. She was brash and a flirt, but she was like that with everyone, even dogs and the odd chickadee. I couldn't read too much into it.

We found a patch of bare dirt and sat down. "Mmmph, that's more like it," she muttered as she spread her legs open for a side stretch. "Nestles the ice right where I need it."

"Morgan, that can't be good for you. You're going to give yourself frostbite."

"You care about my cooch? That's so sweet of you." She tipped her head and winked at me. I felt my own cooch flush. Was she flirting? Or just being her usual brash self?

"I care about all of you. Seriously, I'm looking at your seat height before you get back on that thing."

She reached toward her other leg but kept her eye on me. "So you're telling me your crotch isn't bothering you at all after fifty miles?"

"A little tingly, maybe, but not in pain."

"Good tingly, or bad tingly?"

The fact of her asking made me all the tinglier. "For me to know and you to find out."

"Ooh, I bet it's the good tingly then."

"You know what they say: 'Bicycling puts the fun between your legs.'"

She snickered. "God, I wish."

I went to ask one of the pit-stop volunteers for some string. The guy found a spool of twine and gave me several feet. I brought it back to Morgan, who now lay flat on her back with her legs propped up against a tree trunk. Her water bottle had slipped forward so that it now bulged against the front of her shorts like a monster strap-on.

"Here, take that armadillo out of your pants. I need to take your measurements."

She looked up at me from her spot on the ground. "What for?"

"So I can adjust your seat."

"Don't I need to be on my bike for you to do that?"

"I wanted to spare you the pain for as long as possible."

She smiled with relief and sat up, whipping the water

bottle out of her shorts and nestling against a tree root. "Have I told you lately how much I love you?"

She hadn't. I had never heard her utter the word *love* in reference to anyone, unless you counted the times we'd talked about her realization that she hadn't really been in love with her ex. "No," I said. "But there's a first time for everything."

She looked right into my eyes. "Indeed, there is."

I held the string out to her. "Grab one end and hold it against your inseam. Then stretch out your leg."

She did as instructed, the tip of her index finger pressing down against her chamois, right where the opening between her labia would have been if she'd been naked. I tried not to think too much about that as I pulled the string taut and stretched it to the base of her foot. I crimped my end to mark off the right length. "Back in a flash."

"Uh-uh," she said. "I'm coming with you. I want to watch you in action."

"Think you'll learn a thing or two?"

"Oh, I know I will."

It took us a minute in the maze of trees to remember which one housed our bicycles, but we found them eventually. I took the emergency tool kit out of my saddlebag and used the string to check Morgan's seat height. "Holy crap, no wonder you felt like there was a sledgehammer on your snatch. This thing is at least an inch too high."

Her eyebrows shot up in surprise. "An inch makes that much of a difference?"

"You'll find out in just a second." I used my pocket Allen wrench to lower her seat. The nose was also tilted too far up, so I flattened it out to redistribute the pressure to her sit bones. "Here, get on and see how that feels."

She smirked. "That's what all the ladies say to me."

I held the bike steady as she mounted and pedaled backward to test the feel of the seat without actually moving. "Oh my god. That's so much better. Here I thought my choice was between finishing the ride and obliterating my twat. But this is like . . . butter. Damn, I think my cunt might actually be usable by tonight."

There was no way I could avoid blushing this time. "Are you planning to use it?"

"I don't know. But I like to know it's an option. I guess we'll see what happens when we get to the shore, won't we?" She winked again.

We'd met earlier that summer on one of the training rides. It was my seventh year of long-distance cycling and her first, though she was a few years older than me. Despite the difference in our experience, our cadences were almost identical, so we kept ending up in the same pod of riders. Sometimes the pod dwindled to just the two of us. It was easy to find a rhythm with her and stay in it.

The training rides grew longer as the season progressed, and so did the time I spent with her. She was a great riding buddy, with a million stories to tell and the perfect amount of tough love when I wanted to toss my bike by the side of the road and sleep for the rest of the day—like the grueling ninety-six-degree afternoon in August when she hopped off her bike only long enough to grab the sprinkler off someone's lawn and douse me with it. Her background was in marathon running, and those assholes never give up. A gaggle of nearby kids saw what she was doing and thought it was a hoot. They came running over and accosted us with water Uzis until both of our shirts were soaked through.

God, it felt good when we got back on our bikes. The wind against the wet fabric worked like an air conditioner, and the way Morgan looked in her clinging jersey energized me even more. Normally white, it became almost transparent under these conditions. I could see her skin beneath it and the subtle movements of her back and arm muscles as she steered the bike. When she sat up to ride hands-free on the straight stretches, the outline of her pebbled nipples was unmistakable.

But just because two people have perfect cycling chemistry doesn't mean they'll fit together off the bike. Besides, Morgan had been on a dating sabbatical when I'd first met her, and I wasn't sure if it was over yet.

"How long do you think a person should go without sex after a bad breakup?" she'd asked on our third ride together.

I liked to think she was wondering because of my irresistible wiles, but those kinds of non sequiturs bubble up all the time when two people ride together. There's only so much commentary you can make on the rolling countryside before conversation turns to more personal things.

"I guess it depends," I'd said. "On a person's relationship with sex and how bad the breakup was."

She'd laughed. "I was looking for a pat answer."

"You'll never get a pat answer from me about anything. I'm like Socrates. I turn every answer into a question."

Two weeks before the big ride, she'd dropped this one: "You know what's weird? For the first time in my life, I don't feel the need to be in a couple. At all."

My heart sank. I made a show of carefully inspecting

the paper wrapper of my Italian ice for leaks so she wouldn't see the disappointment written all over my face. "Good for you. So no dating for you ever again?"

She tapped her feet against the sidewalk. The metal cleats on her shoes made a crisp *click-click* against the concrete. "That's the funny part. I don't know. I think I could be happy that way. But sometimes when you realize you don't need something—that's the moment when you're ready to have it."

I wanted that kind of confidence, and when I was on the bike, I had it. Getting to the top of a hill or flying down a crest made me feel like I was king of the world.

But whenever my feet left the pedals for solid ground, I returned to my shy and somewhat awkward self, making weird historical references no one understood and liking bad puns more than anyone should. I never knew what to say or do to show my interest in another woman. I'd always been that way, waiting for someone else to make the first move and giving up when they didn't.

The rest of that September day was perfect: high sixties, a light breeze, and scattered cumulus clouds that made the sun feel refreshing rather than relentless. We got to the shore around four p.m., checked our bikes, and went straight to the beach house we'd rented with a few other riders. We were sharing a room with two double beds.

"How's your pain doing?" I said, beginning to unpack my clothes.

"Much better, thank you. Your seat adjustment worked wonders. My pelvic bone still feels a little bruised, but the fleshy parts are—well, maybe a little tender, but mostly fine." She threw her duffel bag on the bed farthest from the door, pulled out a bathing suit, and started stripping her clothes off. "God, it feels good to get out of these disgusting shorts. It'll feel even better to get into that ocean. It's so invigorating this time of year."

I looked away, but not until after catching a glimpse of her ass. It was my first time seeing it, and it was breathtaking.

"You don't have to avoid looking at me." Her voice came over my shoulder. "I don't think I have anything that will shock you. And if I do, it's better you learn now."

"How's that?" I pulled my bra off through the armholes of my cycling jersey.

"You know, in case I want to sleep naked tonight. Or in case we both do."

I looked over my shoulder toward her, but didn't turn all the way. I didn't have to. There was a mirror on the wall, and I could see all of her in it. Her jersey and bra were off now, leaving only stripes in her skin where the elastic had been. She was still gorgeous. Her breasts drooped slightly under their own weight, their coppery nipples as large as silver dollars.

She met my eyes in the reflection. Was it a challenge? If so, I wasn't prepared for it.

My throat went dry. "I brought pajamas."

She shrugged. "It's up to you."

We threw sundresses over our bathing suits and bought the largest custard cones known to humankind before finding a spot on the beach. We were starving, and since we would be riding back to Philadelphia the next day, we figured we might as well carbo-load now. My stomach grew full and tiredness started to hit me; when I was done with my cone

I lay back and closed my eyes. It felt good, the sun lighting up my eyelids and the sound of the waves in my ears.

When I opened my eyes, the sun was in a different place in the sky and Morgan was leaning over me, whispering, "Wake up, sleepyhead. The last thing you want is a sunburn."

She was so close I could smell the remnants of frozen coffee custard on her tongue. I could smell her sunblock too, and the sheen of sweat she hadn't yet washed off. It reminded me of sex. I wanted to bury myself in it.

"I still have sunblock on," I grumbled, but she was right. If I was going to sleep, it should be back in the beach house.

"Come on." She stood up and grabbed my hand to pull me with her. "The ocean cures everything."

I wasn't so sure about that when, a minute later, I found myself knee-deep in the freezing tide. "Crap, this is cold."

"The perfect thing for tired muscles and a weary groin," Morgan said, lowering herself into the water until only her shoulders and head bobbed above it. Her hair floated around her like seaweed, reminding me of all those drawings of mermaids I used to make when I was a kid and in love with Disney's Ariel, princess of the sea.

Desire flooded me. My calves could barely feel anything thanks to the cold, but the rest of me felt too much. I wanted to kiss Morgan now, under the bright blue sky.

I wanted to do much more than kiss her.

I sank into the water next to her, almost kneeling. The briskness of the water was as shocking as an orgasm. I gasped just as loud.

"I like that sound," Morgan said. She reached for my hand under the water and found it. We linked our fingers.

She leaned in closer. "I'd like to hear more where that came from."

"You're an incorrigible flirt today, aren't you?" I said breathlessly.

"For you? Always." She slipped her hand from mine, ran her fingers along my waist and down my hip, stopping at the top of my thigh. The ocean lifted and rocked us, moving like a heartbeat through both our bodies. As it rose, we rose with it, standing tall. As it receded, we sank, our knees descending into the seabed. "Does it bother you?"

I was too cold to blush. "Only if you don't mean anything by it."

"I mean everything by it." And then, her lips close to my ear, as if her words were too private to even share with the ocean, "We've been beating around the bush, haven't we?"

My brain chose that inopportune moment to notify me of the double entendre of *beat* and *bush*. What was I, twelve?

Measured by sense of humor, yes. I started to laugh. Then tried to stop laughing.

Of course, that just resulted in me laughing harder.

She looked at me, bewildered.

I had to explain myself. I didn't want her to think I was laughing *at* her. "It's funny because beating around the bush is the opposite of what we've been doing. Technically speaking."

Well, that was it. Now she'd know for sure how much of a catch I wasn't. I considered ducking under the water and staying there until I reached the shore.

But then I heard her own laughter, louder than the

seagulls cawing above us. "Well, yeah. If you mean us together. Though, to be honest, I beat around my own bush pretty often."

I didn't think it was possible to get any wetter, submerged in the ocean as I already was. But the image that came into my mind's eye made me flood the lining of my swimsuit. "That's . . . hot," was all I could think to say.

She smiled. "You know what's even hotter?"

I shook my head.

She leaned in and said in that same private voice from earlier, "Lately, the thing that gets me off the hardest is thinking about you."

My clit stood at attention despite the freezing water. I forgot about how tired I was, about the people on the boardwalk who might see us, about the sand that had washed into the back of my suit and made my skin itch. Morgan and the ocean were all I saw and smelled and heard. I looked at the drops of water coalescing on her shoulder, sparkling in the late afternoon sun as if they were giving off their own light.

I kissed one of those drops. It was salty and warm, and Morgan shuddered. "Oh," she said, in soft surprise.

I kissed her mouth next.

Her lips were warm and wind-chapped. She opened them like she was ready to devour me for dinner. She slipped her finger under the opening of my swimsuit.

Up until that moment, I'd forgotten myself along with my tiredness. Maybe that's what had let me be brave enough to kiss her, even though I wasn't on my bike.

But with her finger slipping over my clit, I came back to my body. I was in it, and still unafraid.

I wanted her to devour me.

I moaned something like *yes* into her mouth, or tried to. Our tongues were too tangled for words. She pulled back, just slightly, then pressed her lips to my cheek as she spoke, as if she couldn't bear to separate completely. "I want to taste you."

We ran the whole way. Desire made our bodies forget they'd just ridden eighty miles. We rinsed off together in the enclosed outdoor shower, kissing and clinging as we pulled off our suits and the water poured over us.

"I'm torn between making you come now and waiting until we're inside," she said as she lifted her mouth off my breast.

"Do both." Was that me speaking? Yes. I had become someone else, and I liked it.

She crooked an eyebrow. "Yeah? Can you handle it?"

I spread my legs to give her access to my clit and reached for hers, but she swatted my hand away. "Not yet. Too sore. I'll need something more gentle."

I spoke my deepest desire. "My tongue?"

"Yeah." She pressed her lips to mine, opening her mouth as she stroked two fingers up and down either side of my clit. The water made things tricky, washing most of my lubrication away, but there was still enough that she managed to slide one finger inside me, quickly followed by another. I grunted into her mouth and spread myself wider, propping one foot against the wooden shower wall as my cunt spasmed around her, my breaths shallow and desperate.

She brought her thumb to my clit, swiping it back and forth across the hardened nub. Heat built up in me. I felt like I was going to melt, or explode. I wanted to come, and I also fought against it. The sensation was almost too intense, terrifying and wonderful, like hurtling down a steep, winding road on my bicycle, the wind growing louder in my ears as I built up speed, each slight maneuver the only difference between crashing and soaring.

Our kissing grew messy. She ran her free hand over my wet breast, gave it a firm squeeze as she pressed harder against my clit, and slid a third finger inside me, moaning as if she were the one being touched.

It was the sound that did me in. I sucked her tongue into my mouth and came, wave after wave crashing over me.

"God, you're hot," she whispered against my neck as I tried to catch my breath. "Even better than I'd imagined."

In our bedroom, Morgan said my cunt tasted like honey. I said that was flattering, but probably inaccurate from an objective point of view. Her laugh lit up her eyes.

To me, she tasted like the ocean had seeped into her crevices and was now pouring back out. I worked my tongue around her swollen clit until she begged. "Suck it, Lori, please." She squeezed her thighs against my head in her excitement; I pushed them back open to get better access, bringing her hard nub between my lips and drawing my cheeks in. She cried out—her legs quaking, her clit throbbing against my tongue.

"You can—*oh*, um . . . I . . . mmm . . . I came, you can—"

I looked up and smiled at her. "Keep going?"

Her cheeks and chest were flushed pink, her chest heaving. "I was going to stay you can stop, but since you're offering . . . "

"If it doesn't hurt, I want to keep going."

Her look was perplexed. "Why would it hurt?"

"Your bike saddle?"

"Oh." Her eyes went wide. "Funny, I forgot all about that."

"Good. Let me help you forget some more." I dove back in between her legs.

My pajamas never made it out of my travel bag. We fucked throughout the night and slept less than we should have. Still, when the alarm went off in the morning, I had no regrets.

"How's your crotch?" I couldn't resist asking as we rode off at daybreak. The sun hid behind some low clouds, giving the sky a grayish-pink cast and turning the ocean steel blue as we rode along the shore.

"Never been better."

"Never? You exaggerate."

She pursed her mouth as if she were lost in thought. "No. Definitely not exaggerating. I don't think my crotch has ever been so happy." She glanced over at me. "I'm pretty happy too."

We turned a curve in the road so that the ocean was now behind us. "So you're ready for another eighty miles?" I said.

"Of course." She smiled, and just at that moment the sun came out of hiding. Its light shimmered across her skin. She seemed to be glowing from the inside. "With you, I'm ready for anything."

THE DIARY

Emily L. Byrne

Your diary is sitting out on the table when I get home, a puzzling, mysterious presence glowering at me when I get too close. Just the fact that you keep an actual book for the express purpose of writing down your thoughts and the day's events baffles me. That's why there are blogs, right? Just looking at it intimidates me a little.

Another thought occurs to me. Were you writing about me? What were you saying? I hover over the table, eyeing the book, one hand twitching in an effort not to reach toward the closed cover.

What will happen if I open it? I know you have your secrets, your hidden inner self that you reveal to no one. Well, almost no one. I have seen flickers of it, here and there, when I open myself completely to you, submitting to your will. Only then do I get to see anything like your true self.

I want to see more. And this could be my first real chance. For all your bravado, it can be like coaxing a terrified animal out of hiding to get you to open up. Sometimes, like now, impatience gets the better of me. I want to understand you, to make you belong to me the way I belong to you.

But I have to admit to myself that maybe this isn't the right way to do it.

Besides, if you come home and find me reading your diary, who knows how you'll react? My clit throbs as I contemplate your more creative punishments. Or, much scarier, you could shut me out, close the door on that little bit of yourself that I've managed to draw out, maybe permanently. I don't think I could bear that.

I put my hand in my pocket and turn away from the table, resolution steeling my shoulders.

You will be home from your meeting soon. I could put on something slinky and wait for you in the bedroom, surrounded by lit candles, maybe toss around a handful or two of those synthetic rose petals that I found at the mall. They smelled gross in the tin but not so bad on the bedroom rug.

Maybe I should open a bottle of sparkling juice and pull out some glasses to help set the mood. You told me once that I could keep wine in the apartment if I wanted to, but I don't want to risk your sobriety for something so minor. Besides, I liked the taste of the sparkly stuff better now.

A part of me wants to like everything you like, wants to surrender the minute you touch me, to swoon and faint into your arms like a heroine out of a bad movie. But I know that's not what either of us really wants. I've seen the glint in your eyes when I play hard to get. You like the thrill of the chase, followed by capture and possession. And I do love being captured and possessed.

Maybe I can pick up a few hints about what else you might like. My better self wars with my curiosity for a minute, then two. One of them wins.

An instant later, I'm back at the table with one eye on the clock and the front door. I hesitate, just for a moment, before I flip the book open. Your diary lies open in front of me and I tremble at my presumption. I have to stop myself from trying to pretend that it's just a book, some fantasy or mystery that you left on the table mid-read. I shouldn't distance myself from the level of intrusion that I'm about to commit.

I should . . . I should stop . . . I sink into the chair and grab the book. Then I let your words, written in your precise handwriting, wash over me.

I skip the first third looking for the date when we met. A lot of it looks like it's about your past and things you haven't been willing to tell me yet, and I'm determined to let you keep most of your secrets. I may be having an illicit look at your diary, but a gal's got to have some standards. I keep checking for my name in your meticulously dated pages, flipping faster and faster until the movement hypnotizes me.

Which explains why I don't hear the door open when you come home. I had wandered into what I was looking for, hoping for, and the reality took a minute to kick in. Even after I look up, I can still see your fantasy like a movie playing on the wall behind you. It is a film showing that ends abruptly when I see your expression. Or, rather, your lack of expression.

Oh shit.

My mouth opens like it's on strings but the apologies and the excuses simply aren't showing up the way I hope that they will. And my brain is full of your faded jeans and leather jacket and what might happen if I stripped you right out of them with the power of my desire alone. The ache between my legs hits me hard just then, as does the sudden terror that I'm never going to get to feel your touch again.

"Why?" Your voice is a growl, a snarl that makes me cringe, despite my best intentions to handle this like a grown-up.

"I . . . I . . . " Excuses dance in my head. *I picked it up by accident. I thought it was something else. It fell open.* "I wanted to know what you wrote about us. Me." It sounded so horribly juvenile when I said it that way. I hand over the book and stare at the floor waiting for my punishment, whatever it is, to fall.

You are quiet for a very long time. I shut my eyes, an involuntary gesture, made to shut you out, to shut out my sin. To delay the moment when you kick me out of your life.

"Did you like it . . . the parts that you read?"

My eyes jerk open, sending a sudden wave of heat down to my pussy. I squirm my butt against the chair, thighs suddenly slick and hot and wet with imagining you naked and vulnerable on our bed. Tied down and spread-eagled and wanting, the way you like to have me. Yes, I liked it. I liked it very much.

Even though it scared the crap out of me.

Words well up in an unintelligible noise that falls out of my mouth, so garbled I'm not even sure what they started out to be. I follow them with an emphatic nod and a wide-eyed, apprehensive stare.

I have plenty to be apprehensive about. It isn't like

I've earned your trust. Quite the opposite, in fact. That thought throws ice-cold water on my fantasies. You aren't even looking at me now.

Instead, you're staring at your diary and the expression on your face breaks my heart. "I'm so, so sorry! I love you so much and I'm such an idiot. I didn't mean to hurt you! It won't happen—" You hold your hand up, and I grind to a halt.

You look straight into my eyes, your blue gaze piercing through me, seeing and weighing everything I've done, everything I might do. I bite back a whimper. When you do move, it's like you've read my mind. You take off your leather jacket and drop it on the back of one of the kitchen chairs. Then, you pull off your white T-shirt, exposing your sturdy body, thick muscles overlaid with a layer of soft skin. You pull off your bra, exposing your breasts, and I gasp.

Then you put your damned diary on the table between us. I stare at it and wonder what to do next.

You turn away from me, walking toward the bedroom without a word or a glance back at me. Should I follow you? Should I stay here? Your diary stares back at me from the tabletop like an accusing eye and I stare back, lust and longing and guilt swirling around in my head until there is no room for anything else.

"Hey. In here. Bring the book." You don't say anything more than that, but it's enough. I get up and follow the sound of your voice into the bedroom, letting it pull me along like a leash.

The seven steps to the bedroom give me valuable seconds to compose what I am going to say when I see you. Whatever that may be. To— I turn the corner into the bedroom to find your clothes on the floor and you lying naked on the bed.

You are lying on your stomach and from what I can see in the dim light, every muscle in your body is tense. Your eyes are closed and your paddle lies on the bed next to you.

I stop and stare while I sort my thoughts. Am I supposed to use the paddle on you? Somehow, it doesn't look like you will be having much fun if I do. Even the sight of your naked butt and your spread legs only gets me slightly hot. Okay, maybe a little more than that.

But I want you to want me the same way I want you. I want you to want to surrender to me, if that's what you want. And from this angle, it looks like you are having doubts.

"Baby . . . " I rest a reluctant hand on your calf. You quiver. "You don't have to do this, whatever this is. If anything, I should be lying here waiting to be paddled because of what I did. This feels . . . weird." I run what I hope is a soothing palm up over your back and you shudder.

Instead of replying, you stretch your arms out, gesturing toward the ropes tied to each bedpost. I lean over, stroke your hair. "Why?"

You open one eye. "Do you trust me when it's you lying here?" I nod. "Then show me that I can trust you, too." You growl our safeword like a talisman and close your eyes, exhaling in a long shuddering breath.

I chew my lip, but reach for the cuffs, fastening each to one of your limbs. I check to make sure that their grip on you is firm, not painful or distracting, before rocking back on my heels. In the scene in your diary, you're on the bed just like this and I'm . . . my eye falls on the closet. I'm wearing something more interesting than a cotton skirt and an oversized shirt.

I get off the bed, go to the closet, and select my outfit with care. Then, I walk back to you and run my fingertips lightly from your heels to your shoulder. "I'll be back, babe. Let your imagination run wild for a little while." Then I trail my hand over your ass and send my fingers down your slit, reaching inside to pinch your clit lightly. You reward me with a gratifying gasp and I grin before taking my outfit and going into the other room to change.

A few moments later I'm transformed from zaftig hippy goddess to slutty leather queen. It's amazing how much difference showing more skin and accenting the rest with black leather and red lace can make. I even slip on the high heels that I can only wear for an hour or two before I have to sit and take them off. Tonight, I will be mistress of them as well as you. After a moment's hesitation, I add makeup, making my eyes cloudy and mysterious, my lips a crimson slash across my broad, pale face.

I open the bedroom door again and sashay in, only to be beset with doubts. I should have put a butt plug into your enticing ass or inserted those lovely steel balls that we keep in the silk case next to the bed into your open pussy. Or at least remembered to gag you. I reach for the diary, your eyes on me, and try to page through to the scene you wrote.

"Put the damn book down and get over here." And I start to do just that, right up until I catch a glimpse of myself in the bedroom mirror. A demon queen stares back at me from the shadows of our room. Whatever she is, she's not a gal who just does what she's told, no matter who's doing the telling.

I perch on the chair nearby and continue paging through your diary until I find the scene I was reading when you got home. Then, I read it out loud, pausing and purring out the good bits in my sexiest voice until you start to squirm against the cuffs. I stop long enough to reach for the toy box and pull out our tiniest butt plug and some lube. I get it nice and slicked up and slide it into your tight butthole. You yelp and bite down on the pillow. "I'm not done reading to you yet," I murmur as I bend down and lick your ear.

This time, you mutter a couple of choice words and a suggestion about what you'll do to me when I untie you. Old Me from a mere hour ago would have melted into a puddle and unfastened the cuffs. New Me laughs, swats your butt, and slips a finger into your pussy, only to withdraw it when you push back against it. I lick my finger off, slowly, bending over your face so you can watch, then I go back to my chair and your diary.

I keep reading, at least until your running commentary of groans gets too loud for me to hear myself. Then I get up and tug the ball gag free of its bag. You seldom use it on me so I fumble a bit putting it on and you nip at my fingers, your frustration palpable. But I get it on you at last.

Then I slip my fingers into my panties, dip them into my aching wetness and smear it just under your nose. Your hips buck in frustrated desire as I run my hands down your body, checking to make sure that you're aroused and just for the fun of touching your burning skin.

I read some more, but now I pull one of my boobs

out of its lace enclosure and play with my nipple while I read to you, to us. I make sure that you can see my flesh getting hard under my nails, see my hips shift involuntarily against the chair. Your diary is proving most instructive, at least the parts I've given myself permission to read.

The bedroom reeks of all the sex we're not having yet and I slip my panties off before I go to the kitchen and get us some water, yours in a cup with a straw. I remove the gag so you can drink, then put it back as you start to say something that sounds like a plea. Then, I crouch over you and slide my soaking-wet slit down your back and onto your ass. Stretching back, I stick my fingers into your pussy, pulling them out before you can come, then sticking them inside me.

I realize that it's going to get too difficult to keep reading and I pull my hand reluctantly free of my aching wetness and grind myself into your buttcheeks instead. You are squirming beneath me, body pleading in a thousand different ways for every flavor of my touch. My knee brushes your paddle and I pick it up, giving it a moment's consideration before I flop over to your side and give your ass an experimental whack.

I've never used the paddle before, only been the one experiencing its exquisite torment, and my ass aches in sympathy for what I'm about to attempt to do to yours. I give you a few more smacks, trying to get used to the feel of it in my hand. You groan and your flesh jiggles at the impact. I shove my hand between your legs, thrusting inside you with a sudden motion that makes you howl around the gag. The sound, the scent of your desire: this scene bowls me over until I am driving my hand into you, demanding your orgasm in a way I never dreamt of before.

Your surrender arouses me until I think I'll explode if I don't come soon, and I move so that your thigh is between my legs. I try to rub myself off to the same rhythm that I'm fucking you, but it doesn't quite work and you come first with an explosive series of moans and gasps, soaking the sheets underneath you.

It takes me longer, but at last, I too rub myself to a shaking, yelping orgasm on your leg, sending my juices out to coat your flesh. I reach up and unfasten the gag, worried that your labored breathing means that you might be in trouble. Instead, you grab my wet fingers in your mouth and suck them frantically, your tongue between them and over every bit of my palm you can reach.

Reluctantly, I pull away and tug the butt plug gently free from your hole and drop it into the toy-cleaning bowl that we keep on the nightstand. Then I clamber off the bed and grab the steel balls from their silken nest. They are inside your wet, aching warmth in an instant and you groan at the chill contact against the most intimate portions of your flesh. I know just how you feel, and part of me desperately wants to untie you and switch positions.

But I don't think that I've taken you as far as you want to go, not yet. So I give you another drink of water and pick up the paddle again. This time, I stand up to get a bit more weight behind my swing. You give me an unreadable glance and tense up, so I pause to touch you, to kiss your back and your nearest asscheek. I caress you, even darting my fingers inside to shift the balls around until your moan reassures me that you're ready.

Hoping I am, too, I smack your ass once, twice, then alternate cheeks as I watch your skin turn a satisfying red. You're yelling into the pillow now, writhing and yanking at the ties until I wonder if the bed is going to survive tonight. Not that it matters. I'm enjoying this new side of you, and I want to see more of it.

A few more strokes and I can tell you're getting close from the way that you're breathing. I set the paddle down and reach for your clit, rubbing and circling it in the sea of your juices that I've managed to call up. When you come, it's sudden and even lovelier for that. Your body shudders against me, legs locked, then spasming, muscles twisting, your mouth open in a howl.

I rub until you finish, then withdraw my hand slowly. The aching need between my own legs is getting too intense to ignore, and I don't want to just use your thigh this time. I set you loose, letting you rub your wrists and ankles as I start undressing. But you grab me before I can finish, shoving me onto the bed and riding me with your mouth, your tongue, until I come so hard I think I'm going to black out.

As I gasp my way back into my body, you murmur, "I want you to start keeping a diary."

RELICS

Sarah Fonseca

*With a wide variety of miniature accessories,
a doll hospital, and a hair salon with personal
stylists, they are perhaps among the most luxu-
rious toys ever invented.*

Seven hours. The stale vacuums of the airport, the late
afternoon flight; the asphyxiating incense of the rental, a
car-freshener fir bouncing about on the rearview mirror,
mocking us. When we arrived in that flat town in Georgia,
our tired lungs welcomed big swallows of the clean, wet
air. I could forgive the heat.

Begonia parked by the mailbox to not wake her auntie
with the headlights' glare.

"She does know we're staying here? Right? B?"

Begonia was busy unlocking the entry gate to the gravel
path that led to her childhood home. Her brow remained
furrowed until the lock finally caught.

She didn't answer. I decided that I didn't want to

know. Her posture slumped under the weight of both our suitcases, which she'd insisted upon carrying. Head bowed, her bangs caught in her eyelashes, she blew them away. The rest of her hair became helplessly tangled in the bags' handles. As we approached the clapboard house with the partial second story, I realized that our path was lined by dozens upon dozens of little plants, some with violet flowers, some not, all bearing furry leaves: *begonias*. She wasn't the only one. We weren't the only ones.

The last time I'd felt truly alone with Begonia, we were in her bed in Chicago.

"Come with me," she whined before she took me in her mouth, kneeling above me, back bowed terrifically, a skinny cellar cat of a woman. Whenever she had me like *that*, I imagined her mouth at my nipple. Whenever she suckled at my breast, I envisioned her below. Four hands, four breasts, two wet clefts, two mouths. There never seemed to be enough of us; our fucking was never without a joyful dissatisfaction.

While I too fantasized about shared tremors, I couldn't actually do what she wanted. I was never able to make love like a synchronized swimmer. I became too engrossed in the other's undoing to experience my own at the same time. But I *could* try. The room was pitch-black; there was only one outlet near her bed. Her beloved KORG and a floor lamp, the lone source of lighting in the basement apartment's bedroom, often fought over it. That night, the keyboard won.

I leaned forward and found her opening, appreciating the throb above.

"No, Cacey," she whimpered, moving my hand to her thigh. "I mean, come with me to Valdosta."

"What's in Valdosta?" I managed.

"A wedding. But if I tell you that there's more of *this* in Valdosta, will you join me?" Her tongue teased, nudging folds away, hiding and unveiling me until I was too swollen to be concealed. "I want to lap you up in a thousand states."

"But we've only got fifty."

"Forty-nine now to go, technically."

The comforter became drenched. The sheets were tugged away from the mattress by the rhythm she encouraged. I don't remember when, but I agreed to accompany her. Tagging along to watch her dear old friend hitched was nothing. If Begonia wanted to rob a bank, I would've held its door open for her with a curtsy.

The front door opened creaklessly. Begonia veered to her left, leading me by the hand.

"I don't want to lose you," she said with a whisper and a wink.

I felt the shape of the carpeted stairs beneath my feet. They grumbled under the weight of our bodies and luggage. I prayed that this primitive alarm system, relied upon heavily by the parents of starry-eyed adolescents, didn't apply to thirty-year-olds.

When she reached the top, Begonia pressed the weight of her body into the door, opening it. An intricate stained-glass lamp sat atop a small nightstand, illuminating the room all by its lonesome. I realized that we were in her old bedroom. This was where she grew larger. I imagined her, young and sinless, gazing through that tiny window each night as the sun set over the thicket of poplars. But looking around, I was forced to stifle a giggle. The nightstand was covered with Minnie Mouse stickers. The twin bed's surface was monopolized by decorative throw pillows. Begonia's old room was in a heightened state of feminine conflict, as though its invisible boarder, trapped between girlhood play and womanly opulence, decided she simply *must* have both.

Her Auntie Ethel, she explained, wasn't really her auntie but had taken her in when she was still quite young. Ethel was a busy woman, caught between Clerk of Court duties and odd jobs that Begonia never fully understood. Unlike most parents with an empty nest, Ethel had never found time to empty the room of its juvenile trappings or exchange its twin bed for something more age-appropriate. Unable to find time to subtract, the woman added. She purchased the lamp, miscellaneous accents, and new sheets from Belk. High-thread-count Egyptian cotton—for a child's bed!

My jaw went slack at the sight of three dolls in hoopskirts, clearly not made for playing with, at least during this century, staring blankly at us from a decorative shelf, their ceramic faces impossibly white. Their hair was long, reaching all the way down their backs to their tiny doll bottoms.

"Auntie . . . her tastes . . . I'm sure she thought I'd appreciate their hair, but . . . "

"Is your auntie responsible for that welcome sign hanging at the city limits, too?" I laughed. "*Southern Charm, Not Gone With the Wind.*"

"I'm sorry you had to see these," she sighed, turning each doll 180 degrees so her blanched ceramic nose was pressed against the wall. "They're so pale. You'd think the Southern belle was subjected to cruel experiments in phlebotomy."

I recalled what an American history professor at the University of Chicago once told our class about such toys, specifically those found in the South. One women's college, I believe in North Carolina, celebrated each outgoing senior class with a custom doll, complete with a unique dress. The first Black woman graduated from the university in the early 1970s. As for the dolls, well . . . they remained as white as they'd always been. That seemed to be the persisting slogan of the region, one that seeped into the floor of our old bedroom: *as they'd always been*.

"My stomach hurts."

Begonia was hanging her lavender bridesmaid's dress in the closet between a graduation gown and a prom shift. She didn't pause to look at me, only pointed to a pencil box on her old kneehole desk.

"There's something in there that might help you."

I opened it to find small cotton bullets with shrink-wrapped casings.

"You're so mean." I rolled one of the tampons between my fingers. "These *have* to be expired."

"Cotton doesn't expire, does it?"

"I don't know. *Does it?*" I asked, eying her aunt's dolls. I pelted Begonia with the bullets. We laughed until it became too difficult to breathe again.

As she filed the dress between those of earlier rituals, a wicker basket tumbled from the closet's highest shelf and onto the floor, narrowly missing Begonia's nape. From it spilled palm-sized spheres, hearts, and stars, all made of colorful plastic. Some of them burst open like oysters as they hit the floor, unveiling miniature pastel worlds full of staircases and domestic trappings and, in some instances, the pearl that was a miniature woman who bent at the waist.

Begonia looked to me sheepishly. "Death by Polly. A girl could dream!"

A childhood toy carries as much clout as an old lover, a name that only enters the mind at odd intervals. At separate points in time, both were heartbreakers.

Rather than picking up our toys, we made more of a mess, tossing one another's blouses atop bins of wide-eyed Barbies and our unpacked suitcases. She held me close on that skinny bed, our sides resting against those linens that felt like a white lie. Because my hurt was *for* Begonia, not because of her, it was easily relieved.

Her hands found my body before mine could grip hers. With a grade-school bully's smirk, she pushed her way into me. When I gasped, she covered my mouth with the center of her palm, fingers curling and hooking against my jawbone for support. I liked the threat, the faint possibility of a broken bone. Her hand smelled metallic, like her amplifiers, microphones, guitar strings. The scent of her apartment in McKinley Park was never far behind her. I can no longer remember where, but in her old bedroom, I'd spotted a toy upright piano: the tiniest of unspoken origin stories.

My vision blurred as Begonia fucked me, fingers catching me on the inside as forcefully as they did my face. All I could see was pink in a hundred shades, from the curtains to the dresses of those terrible dolls whose gazes had been censored: carnations, puces, corals. My legs began to tremble. I pulled her from me by the wrist and shoved her down onto her own back.

A wooden placard above the old kneehole desk bore her name. That looping *Begonia,* hand-painted on rosewood. Her name, in her signature color. The one she appropriated during a dirty touch or thought. Like a mouth that supplied its own lipstick. Or the moth, *Anisota stigma*, deepening in hue to blend into a bed of leaves. I spread her knees apart, too far for that tiny bed that we risked spilling from, tumbling to the floor with a groan and a thud that would surely wake Ethel below. *My* rosewood. I longed for the ability to taste colors: before trying, I pressed my cheek to her rise. Cotton, silk . . . all put to shame by flesh.

Begonia, I knew, had been a little girl in that bedroom— she was twelve, fourteen, sixteen. Grown-up sheets, nice though they were, couldn't disrupt my fantasy by perpetuating adulthood. In looking at her that way, I too felt twelve, fourteen, sixteen; a girl who'd been living elsewhere in America, also trapped alone in her room with her *things*. My thoughts possessed the poor tracking of a home movie: What would it have been like to have rescued her? To tiptoe up that narrow staircase and into her bedroom in the dead of night? To have been young *with* the young! A sensation that had eluded me in my own bespectacled youth.

I sat atop her, my bottom moving against her, her—oh, what would Begonia, the unwilling belle on the shelf, have called it *then*? Her private part? Her pee-pee? Her cherry?

"Tell me about the first time you did this to yourself," I pleaded. "It was here in this very room, wasn't it?"

I pictured her years before, the more modest of her two hands caressing her thighs as the other did the devil's bidding. Was the flesh she gripped nicked by the disposable razor she was still trying to master?

She nodded, lip between her teeth. Her head rolled to the side, toward the Minnie Mouse'd nightstand. "I, um, used a hairbrush." She reached down, tapping the drawer where she'd hidden away that particular love. "I was seventeen." She chuckled. "Later than most, I suppose? I started right before I left." She sighed with defeat, as though she couldn't account for lost opportunity.

I didn't respond, eyes closed, imagining her first curious considerations and the cautious thrusts that followed. I recollected those years when the arousal between my legs was so new that it was startling, as though a heaving waterfall had developed in that strip of my cotton panties (and maybe one had, with no intent of ever going dry, romantic droughts be damned). While I loved Begonia *so* when we were cunt to cunt and panting, it was never our bodies' physical symmetries that aroused me. I'd been with plenty of women before her. Women with breasts larger and smaller than my own. Women who, after a lifetime of pained longing, *finally* had access to a pill that allowed them to develop a sweet rise beneath their own nipples. With Begonia, It was *her drip*. Never had I been with anyone who wet herself as she did, as I did. The chicken-and-egg of it all: Which came first? Her wetness or mine?

She slid from beneath me, a strand of her remaining on my thigh. Fearing that I'd upset her with my probing, I kept my eyes clenched shut. I heard a zipper, a rustle. And finally, the creak of the bed and the relief of her warm body on mine. I opened my eyes to her clutching my hairbrush's handle, as hot pink and transparent as I felt.

"Let me do it to you, I want to do it to you so badly, I

want to do it, I want—" She dragged the handle between my legs. Do hairbrush manufacturers *know*, I wondered, what girls do up in their rooms with their creations? Do they have code names used in design meetings for products made in pretty colors that have soft gel handles? Do they wink and elbow one another as they discuss their brushes and their consumer base? Do they allow their own daughters to buy their "handy" masterpieces?

The handle's curious ridges caught and released my clitoris; a finger running across the strings of a harp. My legs spasmed with each pluck. I wanted to ask Begonia to slap me there with the brush's backside, or shove the handle into my mouth and into my cheek, but I knew she'd taunt. I couldn't bear that sort of waiting. I stifled myself to get what I wanted most of all.

She rolled her eyes as I whimpered, its own sort of taunt. I wanted Begonia to hurt me, to bruise me on the inside with my hairbrush. Like we were girls again: new to this, trapped, and reduced to invention.

She took the sticky handle in one hand and my hip with the other. I rolled in the direction of the push, onto my stomach. The flat, transparent side of our new toy came into contact with my bottom, over and over. I choked out a small sob as it hovered over the backs of my thighs. I wanted to kiss the copper-flavored fingers that were in my hair, shoving me mouth-first into an accent pillow's appliqué. She continued the beating, the pink paddle catching the ceiling's light and throwing it elsewhere.

"All right?"

I nodded. Behind the throb of my own pulse, I heard a murmur: "*Good girl.*"

Begonia knew what she was doing; she always did. I

was always the most open to her from behind. She held the bristles in her fist and allowed me to take my brush into me. The tensing of unseen muscle, the slippery acceptance of Begonia and whatever she offered. With my own hands pinned beneath my stomach and breasts, that was what I'd yearned for.

I knew she couldn't hear me, but I screamed for her to go as deep as the hairbrush would allow. Finally, she pulled it out, shoving it back in with a sigh of her own. Begonia removed her hand so that she could watch. I obliged until her arms gave out and my body couldn't do anything else but banish her.

Nothing was pink anymore; everything was red. My sight took on the color of the scarlet vessels in my eyelids. Though blinded, I knew Begonia was grinning, her cheeks flushed. I could hear it in her breath, those occasional giggles I associated with playgrounds. Hers was nothing like the gaunt faces of those ceramic dolls, sheltered from the sight of us.

She discarded the brush on the Minnie nightstand and sought me out with her mouth. When I first saw Begonia onstage, I'd grown light-headed: she was pulling her mouth into shapes I'd never fathomed, emitting alarming wails that one just doesn't hear—and isn't supposed to hear—in a hazy punk venue like Subterranean. I wanted to see who was making those sounds! I'd grappled around men three times my size to catch a glimpse. And there she was.

There I was. With a meek thrust of my hips, I gave out against her tongue. Begonia's fingers, filthy as ever, went on to tease the fat brass bead at the end of the misplaced lamp's chain.

FINE LINES

M. Birds

Alice Courtney is beautiful when she cries.

Sofía's never seen anything like it, the way the woman can go from pleasantries to tears the moment the slate's out of frame. Is that sort of pain always there inside her—is everything else just acting? Or is it all the same—crying on camera, laughing with her costar, smiling wryly at Sofía in the mirror. ("Make me look like Angelina Jolie, will you?")

That's why you never date actors, no matter how soft-skinned they are. They don't know when to stop pretending.

"Cut," Fernando calls. "Alice, that was perfect. We're going to do one more for sound, okay? Whose idea was it to set us up by a fucking seaport? Reset."

Sofía runs out of the darkness, lugging her makeup kit. The lights are scalding, and she's aware of dozens of eyes on her as she kneels in front of Alice, blotting up her tears.

She doesn't say anything. Alice wouldn't notice if she did. She's still in the scene, and Sofía stares up at her vacant gaze while she powders away the shine.

"Back to ones," the assistant director shouts, and Sofía goes back to the sidelines to watch the next take, leaving her whole heart—stupid, wasted organ that it is—there, beneath the lights.

The first time she sees Alice, her face is a reflection in a mirror. She is probably what—forty-five?—and looks younger than she does onscreen, and smaller. Most celebrities are tiny when you see them in real life, and Sofía has been on enough shows to know that the camera is capable of telling all sorts of lies to its audience, sweetly and wet-lipped.

Sofía is thirty, just starting out in the industry, and wouldn't be anywhere near this film if Fan hadn't gotten drunk at a mixer and pissed off the director.

"Are you the new girl?" Alice asks, barely turning her head. "I'm sorry I look so tired today. A bad canvas."

"That's really not fair." Sofía struggles for a response. "If you're a bad canvas, what chance does that give the rest of us?"

The older woman laughs. That laugh is the absolute worst—low and throaty and a bit shy. It makes Sofía feel like spring: all blossoming pink petals and damp grass.

"I bet you say that to all the old women," Alice says, and Sofía orders herself to *keep it the hell together*. By and large, she does. The show is a success, and she leaves the wrap party with her heart in her throat and a sizeable chunk of her student loans paid off.

It's about five months later—she's just wrapped an indie

shoot—when her phone rings. The number is blocked but the voice is completely, horribly familiar.

"Is this Sofía? It's Alice, do you remember me? From *Open the Door*?" Her self-deprecating little laugh makes Sofía close her eyes. "I got your number from a producer, I hope that's okay. I was wondering if you'd go to France with me?"

At this, Sofía's eyes open.

"Sorry—what?"

"I'm starting on a coproduction in about a month. It's not much notice, but I thought we worked well together. I've watched some of the footage and I look better than I have in years." She laughs again, a bit embarrassed. "What do you think? Are you already spoken for?"

If Sofía had been spoken for she would have razed the earth to get out of it.

"No," she says.

"No?"

"I mean, no, I'm not spoken for. Yes, I'll go to France."

"Well. That was easier than I expected."

If this were a movie, it would be the first scene. Sofía saying 'yes.'

They're finished after three more takes. Sofía takes off Alice's makeup, cotton pads swiping slowly over her skin. She never touches Alice's face with her hands unless it's to hold it steady or tilt her chin. Even then, she asks first.

"Look at these crow's feet." Tears are still drying on Alice's cheeks. "Did you know that Elke is twenty years younger than me? Twenty. And I'm supposed to be her grandmother."

Alice is past fifty now; that's a lonely time to be a woman in Hollywood. There are fine lines around her eyes that concealer can't hide, no matter how much Alice wished it did. Sofía spends her days staring into Alice's face, and thinks she looks the same as the day they met. Alice is perpetually auburn-haired and laughing slyly toward the mirror. The lines around her eyes look like a scrawl of poetry.

"You've got an eyelash on your cheekbone." Sofía picks it up with her cotton pad. "You have to wish on it. Like this. You have to blow it off the back of your hand."

Alice sighs but obediently holds out her hand. She looks at the eyelash for a long time before closing her eyes and exhaling. Sofía studies the perfect O of her mouth.

"Shall I tell you what I wished for?" Alice asks, opening her eyes.

"No." Their faces are close together. "If you do, it won't come true."

If this were a movie they would kiss, Sofía thinks. The moment hangs between them like a held breath.

"All right, I'll keep my secrets. But," Alice smiles, "I will tell you if it comes true."

It's not meant to be flirtatious. Alice does not flirt, and she definitely does not flirt with Sofía. They've known each other for too long now, and Alice only ever dates men.

Would the story be the same if she weren't under constant scrutiny, if there weren't cameras on her every waking moment?

Wishful thinking, maybe. Either way, it doesn't matter. The cameras aren't going anywhere. Neither is Sofía.

* * *

Their second film together gets Alice a Golden Globe nomination. Sofía does her makeup for the ceremony, then goes home to watch the show with a girl she met at some awful lesbian dance. When the camera cuts to Alice in the audience, Sofía tries to stop her heart from glowing red-hot with affection, shining through her skin.

"That's the white chick you work for? I thought she'd be younger."

Alice doesn't win, but no one looks as good as her that night. No one. Even the idiot press write up some articles about "aging fabulously" with Alice's face plastered all over them.

Sometime around midnight, after Sofía has just gone to bed, her phone rings.

The number is blocked.

"Hmm, Sofía?" Alice's voice is soft.

"Alice? I'm sorry about—"

"Hush, I'm not calling to—to commiserate. It's an honor to be nominated, isn't that what I'm supposed to say?" Alice laughs, and that laugh in Sofía's bed is not the association she needs to maintain a professional relationship.

"I just wanted to thank you for—tonight. Everyone was so complimentary. And I wondered . . . " Alice sighs, a sigh that Sofía feels through the phone, ruffling the hairs on the nape of her neck. "I wondered if you wanted to do this sort of thing again. There's awards season first, and I'm supposed to go to Prague in April, and I'd like it if—" Alice stops abruptly. "I'm sorry, I've had some champagne."

Sofía has got to be rational about this, reasonable.

Gorgeous women don't just call her up and ask her to go to Prague with them. There must be some downside to all this, some risk.

Her bedroom is glowing, the ember in her chest shining out through her throat.

Oh. There's the risk. Right there.

"Are you asleep?" Alice asks quietly.

Screw the risk, Sofía decides. She'll take it.

They're in Dubai, filming a terrible midlife crisis romance, when Alice asks Sofía why she decided to go into makeup.

No one's ever asked her that. Not even her family. Maybe they just assumed it was a natural progression from *chola* cat's eyes and big hair to putting gloss on celebrities.

Since Sofía's never been asked the question, she's never told this story.

"My *mamá* was glamorous. Real old Hollywood glamour. We didn't have money or anything, but she sure looked like we did. She had this tiny bottle of perfume, what was it—Fleur de Rocaille. She used it so sparingly, just the tiniest drop every day. I don't think she ever finished it."

Even halfway across the world, Sofía can still smell that damned perfume. Lilac, mingled with the scent of whatever her *abuela* was cooking, and her brother's Old Gold cigarettes, and the rot behind the walls of the bathroom.

Her *mamá* made mundanity seem beautiful.

"When she got sick, I was maybe—seventeen? For a while she could do it all herself, but then she got so tired. I started working it out, you know—how to make her skin glow during chemo, how to make her eyebrows look natural. And when I was done she would look in the mirror and smile, maybe for the first time all day. Even at the end."

Alice is watching her in the mirror. Sofía wonders if this is the part of the movie where she's supposed to cry, the big moment where she reveals her tragic story and breaks down. But thinking about her *mamá* doesn't make her sad. Angry sometimes, but not sad.

"I know it's all a trick, right? Women and makeup. I know that what we look like shouldn't matter as much as it does, and it shouldn't have mattered to my *mamá* when she was dying for Christ's sake—"

"You don't have to explain it," Alice interrupts. "It made her happy."

"It did." Her *mamá* wasn't a saint (and had briefly thrown Sofía out of the house after finding her in bed with her first girlfriend) but most of the bad bits fade. The good bits linger like Fleur de Rocaille.

"Why did you go into acting?" she asks. Alice laughs the way that makes Sofía feel like there's no gravity; she's out in space and everything is starlit.

"It's down to my first husband, really," Alice says, looking fondly into the middle distance. "He said that I was only really good at two things: pretending to be someone else and lying. And I thought, well, he knows me best."

Alice has been married twice. Three years to an actor (deceased) and six years to a writer (still friends.) Sofía could have learned all this from a quick Google search. There are other things she knows that she likes to think are private— secrets between her and Alice alone. She knows the way that Alice likes her coffee, and the stupid things that make her laugh. She knows Alice just started wearing glasses, and likes modern poetry but not Shakespeare ("There have been other writers throughout the fullness of time—some of them were even women.") She's been to Alice's home, sat in her bedroom, held her Emmy, petted her dogs. She knows that Alice is terrified of becoming irrelevant, just as much as she is openly furious about Hollywood's treatment of anyone that isn't a straight white man.

Sometimes Sofía wishes she didn't know as much as she did.

Alice knows that Sofía has never been married, has drifted through a series of girlfriends that never seem to stick. (Alice does not know that Sofía's last girlfriend shouted that she'd "never live up to Alice fucking Courtney!" before slamming the door behind her. Alice does not know that Sofía hasn't been in a real relationship for the past two years.)

"Make me look like Penelope Cruz, all right?" Alice asks, and Sofía would say yes to this a million times over. Even if she had known how it would turn out, she would still say yes.

"I've got something for you," Alice says as Sofía is cleaning her brushes. It's Alice's last day on set; the film will wrap within the week. "In my bag, will you get it?"

Sofía reaches into Alice's massive handbag to find a small box.

"What is this for?"

"Don't you know?" Alice smiles enigmatically. "Our anniversary. Ten years since our first film."

Ten years? That can't be.

"I can see you doing calculations in your head. Yes, it's

true. Can you believe it? We're old women now. Well, not you." Alice eyes the package in Sofía's hand. "Open it."

"I didn't get you anything."

"Don't even think on it. It's not much but—it's probably silly."

Sofía opens the box. Inside it is a glass bottle filled with an amber-colored liquid. The air suddenly smells like lilac.

It's Fleur de Rocaille. *Mamá*'s perfume.

Alice is watching Sofía intently. "It's from the 1950s. I thought that might be her era. I've been assured it was stored correctly."

"It's—" How does that sentence end?

It's the most thoughtful gift anyone has ever given her. She feels like laughing and crying, and in a moment born of pure hysteria and aching gratitude, she puts her hand on Alice's face.

Alice's skin is warm. Her lips part as Sofía kisses her, and there is a hint of tongue against Sofía's upper-lip—

—before Alice says, "No."

Sofía pulls away so quickly she almost falls over. Alice is flushed, looking at the floor. She has lifted a hand to her mouth but is not touching her lips.

"That's—not why I gave you that. Not so you would—you don't have to—"

"Oh my god, I am so sorry," Sofía begins. This is what dying must feel like; all the blood in her body has turned to dust.

"Don't apologize. I should have thought—"

"No, it's my fault."

"You—you are much younger than me." Alice still isn't looking at her. "I'm essentially your employer. It isn't a good idea."

"I'm so sorry," Sofía says again.

"Please stop saying that." Alice looks up then, not at Sofía, but into the mirror. "I've gone horribly red. I think I'll—just step outside for a moment. Until—to collect myself."

Then she's gone. And Sofía is kneeling on the ground holding a bottle of perfume in her hand, wishing that the world would end.

Alice is very polite afterward. That's almost worse. They part ways with a handshake, and Sofía resists the urge to drive into oncoming traffic.

Alice doesn't go to the wrap party, and Sofía doesn't see her for three months.

She's just gotten back from her brother's when the phone rings.

Sofía's had a couple of glasses of wine that night, but now she realizes she hasn't nearly had enough.

The number is blocked.

"Alice?" she says as she answers, desperate to be right.

There is a nervous laugh on the other end, and Sofía thinks she might faint or throw up.

"I'm so sorry to call like this, I—I've been thinking about—"

"About?"

"Um. You." Alice clears her throat. "And how we never said a proper good-bye. I handled it all terribly but I think perhaps I was too hasty before. I—panicked, really and I was hoping . . . "

"Where are you? Right now?" Sofía is ready to pay any amount of money for a cab if it means they get to have this conversation in person.

"I'm—this is so embarrassing but I'm actually—outside. Could I come in? Do you think? To talk."

Sofía almost trips in her haste to get down the stairs and throw open the front door. Alice is wearing a tweed coat with the hood pulled up, and her hair hangs in wisps across her forehead.

"I've reconsidered," Alice says.

"Reconsidered?"

Alice looks uncharacteristically anxious, pulling her coat tighter around her shoulders. "If that's even an option now."

It hits Sofía like a bullet. "You have to say yes first. Before I'll—"

"Yes, that's what I'm saying. Yes . . . "

Sofía kisses her before she can finish the sentence. Alice tastes the same, coffee and cinnamon, but this time her hands rest tentatively on Sofía's waist, and she moans quietly into Sofía's mouth.

"Inside," Sofía says because at least one brain cell is still functioning and Alice Courtney should not be seen making out with strange women. Even if Sofía's not strange at all. Even if she knows the pattern of lines around Alice's eyes.

They stumble up the stairway, and Sofía keeps her hands to herself until her door is closed behind them. Then she backs Alice up into it and tugs her coat off her shoulders.

"You have to tell me what to do," Alice gasps as Sofía bites kisses up her neck.

The words sink in. Sofía pulls back, just slightly.

"I've never—with a woman. I've always wanted to. Always, since I was—don't look at me like that."

"Like what?"

"Like I'm experimenting or confused or—I can't think, kiss me again."

Sofía does, licks into Alice's mouth, starving for the way she tastes. She's never been this crazy to kiss someone, never felt this out of control. The coat is pushed to the ground.

"Tell me," Alice whispers, and Sofía hears something else behind her words, under the uncertainty. Need.

"Take off your shirt," she says quietly, and notices the way Alice's pupils dilate.

Alice unbuttons her shirt. She's wearing a beige lace bra and her stomach is soft. Sofía feels a want as sharp as pain inside her.

"Undo your pants."

Alice does. They slide off her waist and rest on her hips.

"Do you like this?" Sofía murmurs, sliding her lips against Alice's neck. "Do you like me telling you what to do?"

"Sofía—"

"I'm going to touch you now, all right? I'm going to put my hand in your underwear and slide my fingers into you. Do you want that?"

Alice shudders a reply, and Sofía traces her hand up Alice's inner thigh before pushing her underwear aside. Her pubic hair is wiry and wet, and Sofía strokes between her lips, coaxing with her fingers until Alice arches her back and makes a lost, fluttering sound.

"Oh . . . your hand . . . "

"Like that?"

"Like . . . yes, like that."

"You're so wet. Do you feel how wet you are for me?"

"Yes, oh yes."

"I want you to . . . " Sofía has to catch her breath because there are so many things she wants right now. "I want you to take the rest of your clothes off and lie down on the bed. I want to look at you."

Alice moves away from the door, shedding clothes as she makes her way to the bedroom. Sofía follows her, eyes lingering on the curves of her hips, her calves, her back. Alice lies down on the bed, chest heaving.

"I'm going to suck on your nipples," Sofía says, crawling across the bed to tongue at them while Alice writhes beneath her. Alice's breasts are perfect, bigger than Sofía could fit in her hands, and she's been dying to touch them for longer than she can remember.

"I'm going to taste you now," Sofía says, placing searing kisses down Alice's breastbone, stopping again to lick and bite at her nipples before continuing down her stomach. Alice flinches as Sofía bites into her pubic hair, tugging gently at it with her teeth.

There are strands of gray in it. The streetlights turn them silver.

"Do you want this?" Sofía asks.

"Yes, before I die!"

"Wrap your legs around my neck." Sofía buries herself in the warmth of Alice's thighs and the taste of her wet cunt. Sofía has always loved the taste of women, but she never felt like she might come just going down on someone, never felt like she was touching herself by touching someone else. Alice shouts at the first lick of Sofía's tongue, tugging her closer with her thighs, pleading for more. She's so wet her thighs are dripping, and Sofía has two fingers inside of her before Alice even realizes what she's doing. She cries and jerks her hips, riding Sofía's hands and face in desperate, shaking movements.

"Oh, oh, oh," Alice breathes in time to the thrusts of Sofía's fingers.

Sofía adds a third finger and Alice tugs at her hair, thighs trembling against Sofía's shoulders.

"You're going to make me—oh god, I'm going to—"

She clenches around Sofía's fingers, a wail rising out of her throat that seems to never end, building and building as she shakes and rocks against her, crying out profanities that Sofía never in her wildest dreams thought she'd hear from Alice Courtney. She wonders if anyone else knows how filthy she is, how she likes to be ordered around, what she tastes like.

At last Alice collapses back against the bed, arms stretched out on either side. Sofía rests her face against Alice's stomach, breathing. She wants to come, wants to touch herself or tell Alice to touch her, but the ache is pleasant right now. A good sort of pain.

"That was . . . " Alice says, as Sofía licks her fingers. "I want . . . "

Sofía kisses her stomach again, then her breasts, then her shoulder (which makes Alice giggle and squirm a bit. Is she ticklish there? This will need investigating).

"I want to touch you too."

"Yes. Just a second." Sofía kisses her, openmouthed and greedy. Alice squeezes her eyes shut.

"I think maybe—maybe I've always wanted this. And I was just too afraid. And then—I met you."

She laughs, the laugh that made Sofía lose her heart, all those years ago.

"Come to Barcelona with me."

If this were a movie, it would be the last scene. The room striped gold with lamplight, the bedsheets white and rumpled. Sofía saying, "Yes."

THE SALE OF TWO TITTIES

Nanisi Barrett D'Arnuk

It was the worst of times. It was the best of times. Oh dammit, who am I kidding? It was definitely the worst time I'd ever had. It seemed like nothing was going right, hadn't been for months. I felt I was drifting: no focus, no plans, nothing interesting. I did my job, got a little exercise, ate the minimum amount of food necessary, and slept. Not much more than that.

I walked down the river walk quite often, sometimes during the day to breathe fresh air and feel the sun on my face, sometimes at night so I could melt into the shadows and watch. People seemed to sense that I didn't want to talk to anyone. I'm very careful about letting anyone into my personal space. No one ever dared to infiltrate my world. No one even tried.

Not that I can't be sociable; I can be the life of the party when I choose. But not today, not this week, probably not this year. I supposed I'd have to get over it someday.

It was a good thing I could work from home. I set my

own hours, worked when I felt like it, and slept when I didn't. I mailed the advertising layouts to the head office and they deposited money into my account. I didn't have to be polite. I didn't have to dress up. I didn't have to do anything if I didn't feel like it.

I guess I'd been this way since Janey walked out on me three months before. I still don't understand what happened. Maybe I was in denial, maybe it was my fault, but I never saw it coming. Pam knew. She and her partner even loaned Janey money to get another apartment. I never realized it until she was gone. By then it was too late.

I would watch the water taxis ferry tourists to the boutiques and cafes along the river. The boutiques where the items cost a lot more than they were worth, but the little sticker on the bottom, with the city's name, said they were purchased in a place that would impress those back home. I wasn't impressed. But then, nothing seemed to impress me these days.

Sometimes I would sit on a bench (I thought of it as *my* bench) and throw bread to the ducks that paddled along the river. I also dropped popcorn onto the grass along the walk for smaller birds and squirrels. They never said thank you, but I knew they appreciated it.

Night was much better for me. I could hide then. Not behind walls or fences, but right out in the open. People never notice anyone in the dark, unless they're paranoid or looking for someone or something. No one peered into the shadows. They usually only saw their companions, enjoyed the cloak of privacy the darkness seemed to offer, and hoped no one would notice them. The cloak was a solo garment for me.

That night, I was pacing like a caged animal, unable to sit still on my bench. I had to move. So, I walked up the mile-long river walk, and then retraced my steps. Maybe the physical exercise, combined with fresh air, would tire me and I'd be able to sleep that night without nightmares and recriminations.

Finally I decided I needed something to help, and walked up the river walk until I reached a side street. Right around the corner was a small bar that didn't seem too crowded and wasn't bright and noisy, an older bar without a glitzy exterior. The facade hadn't been painted in several years. It seemed hidden from the rush of partygoers, only attracting the serious local drinkers who weren't looking for parties, to get laid, or even to flirt. Those who simply wanted a glass of something to take the edge off. My kind of people.

Inside, I looked around. Older patrons sat at tables in the dim light and chatted softly. There were only a couple dozen people. The music was low, the atmosphere just what I was looking for.

I sat on a stool at the bar. Sitting at a table might seem like I was looking for company.

The bartender was a pretty woman about my age and my height, maybe a little thinner. She had medium-brown hair barely brushing her collar and the most captivating soft dark-blue eyes, but I didn't dare stare into them very long. It might have looked like I was interested.

"Scotch," I ordered. "Neat."

"Single malt or blended?"

"Single."

She reached for a glass and a bottle from the next to top shelf and poured a shot. The bottles had one of those special caps that measure the liquor so you don't have to use a shot glass. It also makes sure the bartender isn't being too generous. She smiled when I paid and laid down the tip but didn't say anything, merely picked it up, slid it into her pocket, and walked to another part of the bar. I like that type of bartender. I don't need someone in my business. If I wanted a psychiatrist I'd go to one.

There was something about her, though. I looked up from time to time to watch for a moment, but not too long, so she wouldn't think I was asking her to talk to me. I glanced up once when she took some longnecks to one of the tables. Nice ass, I thought, as she walked across the floor. Moves nicely. The whole package wasn't bad at all. Then my eyes returned to my drink.

I was contemplating my glass when someone sat down beside me.

"Can I buy you another drink?" His voice had a medium range and tone. Nothing distinct about it.

"Nope." I didn't look up to see who he was.

He'd been drinking. I could smell the beer on his breath as he leaned closer with each question.

"Did you see the ball game tonight?" he asked.

"Nope."

"It was pretty good, but Thomas blew it in the sixth inning. You like baseball?"

"Nope."

"Bet you're a hockey fan," he tried.

"Nope."

"Do you ever say anything besides 'nope'?"

"Nope."

"Ah! Playing hard to get."

Nope, I thought. *Being hard to get.*

He talked . . . and talked . . . and talked, trying anything that might get my attention. Sports, the weather, politics . . . just about everything. I was glad he hadn't started up on religion. That would have been the final straw. I'm not sure I'd lost my faith but I didn't want to talk to anyone about it.

So on he talked. Still I ignored him, hoping he'd get the message, not surprised when he didn't. I looked up to see the bartender, not far away, washing a couple of glasses under the bar, listening surreptitiously to the conversation. I gave her a quick, disgusted shrug.

"You want another drink?" he finally asked. "It's almost closing time."

"I doubt it," I finally answered, still staring into my glass. I took another sip of my scotch.

"You doubt you want a drink? Or you doubt it's almost closing time?" He chuckled. I didn't have to look up to see the smarmy smile on his face. I could tell he thought he was funny.

My silence seemed to arouse him.

"Want to go for a walk, then?" he asked, almost whispering in my ear.

"You couldn't afford it," I replied slowly, looking over into his face for the first time. It wasn't the money I was referring to. It was the psychological abuse I was getting ready to heap on him if he didn't go away.

That quieted him for a moment. "You a pro?" he asked, his eyes wide.

That was all I needed to hear. I was tempted to say "No, a dyke," but that would have opened even more items for conversation and I wasn't in the mood.

I turned to him and looked him up and down. I didn't smile.

"If you don't get out of my face," I whispered to him, "I'll yank it out, cut it off, and ram it down your throat."

He didn't ask what "it" was but his attitude seemed to change. I guessed he finally got the message.

"Jeez! I'm just trying to be friendly, just trying to be nice." He looked around as if others were going to come to his defense.

I downed what was left in my glass, half turned, and slapped my hand down onto his leg, barely millimeters from his crotch.

He sprang back instantly. The stool tipped over as he almost fell backward. He struggled to regain his balance.

He looked at me with indignation. "Bitch," he spat. Then he stalked out the door, muttering obscenities that might have angered someone who cared. He almost ran down the walk.

When I turned back to the bar, the bartender was in front of me. "Thanks," she said, and washed off the counter where he'd sat. She reached to the top shelf and poured me anther drink.

"My treat," she said, placing it on the cardboard coaster in front of me. "I've been trying to get him out of here for a week. I was this close . . . " she held thumb and forefinger very close together, "to calling the police." Then she chuckled. "I like the way you did it better. The look on his face was worth the wait."

I toasted her with the glass. "Thank you," I said. She smiled at me, then picked up a dishrag and went to wipe down another part of the bar.

A few minutes later she was back. I didn't look up but I could feel her looking at me. I let her stand there while she washed and dried several glasses. When I did look, she smiled and didn't look away. I stared back down into my glass. I could feel her carefully polishing the glasses.

"Anything else I can get you?"

I had to grin at that one. There were many things she could get me but I wasn't sure I was ready to go that route yet. I just shook my head.

She leaned over the bar to whisper to me, "I heard you tell him he couldn't afford you." She cleared her throat as she looked around to see if anyone was listening. "Think I could?"

I looked up into her eyes in surprise. They were warm, smiling, and inquisitive. I couldn't quite understand their expression. Was that a challenge? An offer?

"Maybe," I answered, not wanting to commit myself. "A lot closer than he could." I didn't want to close any doors yet. I like aggressive women; someone who knows what she wants. "Is this a down payment?" I motioned toward the glass of scotch and for the first time in weeks, I really smiled.

She stepped back and contemplated her next move. "I'll be through here in a few minutes," she finally said. "You should smile more often. It's very nice." She picked up a bar rag and a tray and went to bus the tables that still had clutter on them. There was only one table of customers left in the bar. I sat back and watched her.

Would she follow through? Would I?

I don't know why I went with her, but I did. Was it her eyes? Her smile? Her body? She intrigued me. No needless chatter. No unnecessary games. Just a smile and a look. When she scanned my body, I felt a sudden spasm in my stomach. It dropped down below my belly. I hadn't felt this in several months. When she held out her hand, said, "Come home with me," and motioned me to join her, I clasped her hand and we walked away from the bar.

Her apartment wasn't far up the river walk. As we entered, she turned on a dim lamp near the couch and tossed the mail from the box in the lobby onto a table near the door. The complex had only been finished a year or two so everything was still new. She'd furnished the apartment sparsely but with class. The couch and chair were chocolate brown with dark wooden arms. The coffee table matched.

She drew back the long drapes lining one wall, revealing a small balcony overlooking the water taxi mooring. The view was stunning. At this time of night, the best parts of the city glowed over the small park and the water.

"Nice view," I commented, as she unlocked the sliding glass doors.

"It's one of the few things that make up for the high rent." She slid open the glass door and went out. I followed. We both looked out onto the water for a few minutes, not speaking; we hadn't said twenty-five words since we left the bar.

"It's a beautiful night tonight, isn't it," she ventured without looking at me.

"It's that time of year," I answered, for lack of something intelligent to say. I guessed I was out of practice at this. I couldn't believe I'd just said that.

She smiled at me and we stood there for a few more minutes. I figured my attempt at conversation had fallen short of its mark.

"Let me go slip into something more comfortable," she said as she walked into the bedroom.

I followed her. "Wouldn't the bed fit that bill?" I asked.

She turned and looked at me. "Are you always so direct?"

"Probably." I smiled. "I have a short attention span. I have to say what I'm thinking, or I'll forget."

She was within arm's reach, so I extended mine and drew her to me. She didn't balk at my bold advance, but slowly slid into my arms as though she belonged there.

I kissed her. It seemed like it had been so long since I kissed anyone, I mean, *really* kissed anyone. I'd forgotten how good a woman's lips could feel. They were warm, soft, and pliant. Something I could sink into very easily.

I hugged her into me as she returned the kiss. She seemed to think it was a nice feeling, too. Her tongue finally found its way into my mouth, so I caressed it with my own until she withdrew it.

"You don't say much, do you?" she whispered, grinning at me.

"I like to save my energy for other things."

"I see." Taking a step back, she started to unbutton my shirt. I don't wear a bra. My tits aren't that large, but they're firm, so they stand up by themselves. A bra seemed like a waste of material and money. I haven't worn one in years.

"How much will these cost me?" she asked, cupping my breasts in her hands and running her thumbs over my nipples.

I thought about it for a minute. What could I say? "Best offer," was all I could think of.

"For both of them?" she asked, looking up into my face.

"Yes," I answered. "They're a matched set."

"One time only, or multi-use?" she asked, a sly smile on her face.

"One time," I said carefully. No sense in ruining the moment with assumptions. "But the contract's renewable if the conditions are right."

"I can afford that." She smiled and pushed my shirt off my shoulders.

It was then that she saw my tattoo, a phoenix on my left tit. It rises out of the ashes just above my areola and ascends, surrounded by a fireball, to just over my collarbone. Some of the flames extend over my shoulder.

"Beautiful," she said, fingering the design. "You shouldn't hide it."

"Recently, there hasn't been anyone I wanted to see it."

"Someone should see it every day." She looked up into my eyes with a look so seductive that I felt like I might melt onto the floor right there and then.

I unbuttoned her blouse.

Her bra was so lacy I couldn't understand what was holding her beautiful breasts up. As I finished undoing it, they fell into my hands. They were a good C-cup, very full and firm. Her nipples were erect and hard. I looked at them, running my thumbs slowly over the dark, berry-like nubs, wanting to draw them into my mouth. I'm not sure what stopped me.

While I stood there, entranced by her breasts, she reached for my fly and pushed my jeans toward the floor. She ran her hand over my hips. I don't wear panties, either. I never thought they were comfortable. It's just as easy to wash jeans as it is to wash underwear.

When she glanced down at my body the smile on her face lit the room.

She sat on the bed to untie her shoelaces, took off her heavy sneakers, then dropped her trousers and kicked them aside. I kicked off my loafers and stepped out of my jeans as she slid back onto the bed. I followed, removing her panties as she lifted her hips. We were now clad only in our socks.

She reached for my breast and gently drew it into her mouth. Oh god! It'd been so long. I'd forgotten the feeling. A nip of her teeth, the gentle glide of them running over my nipple, brought me back to the present.

I seemed to lose my strength and rolled onto my back, pulling her over on top of me. In all that movement, she didn't miss a beat, her mouth firmly ensconced on my breast, her tongue and teeth doing marvelous things to my nipples. I hadn't been this aroused in ages.

I could only grasp her back and shoulders. Her skin was soft and smooth. My body was hot and craving; I hadn't felt this much woman-flesh in a very long time. She was trim, not as muscular as I thought she'd be after lifting all those trays of drinks, but I could feel the strength there.

I'm not sure how long she feasted on my breasts but it seemed like hours. I was ready for her. I was ready for anything.

With her mouth fondling my breasts, her hand roamed down my body until her fingers found my center. I was almost crazed. The smoldering embers below my belly threatened to burst into flames at any moment.

Whatever her fingers were doing I didn't want them to stop. Ever.

Sensations overcame me before I even realized it. I closed my eyes, pressed my head back into the bed, and lost track of time. Breathing became an effort, so I didn't even try. Shards of lightning and thunder were running through me.

My body closed tightly around her fingers as shock after shock of orgasm shook me. Someone was screaming. Was it me? As her hand withdrew I came again, even harder.

We rested while I slowly gained control of my breath. She crawled back up beside me.

"Are you all right?" she asked, softly.

It took me a minute. "Very."

After just a moment I suddenly wanted more; more of everything.

I pushed her up, rolled her onto her back, and took a breast into my mouth, sucking in as much as my mouth could hold, then backing off to take her nipple between my teeth, feasting on it until the entire area was puckered hard. What a wonderful piece of flesh! Was the other like this? I moved over to see.

"Is this what you save your energy for?"

"Exactly. I may have to give you a refund."

I kissed and licked down her body, my hand leading the way, reaching down until I felt heat and a hairy patch. I felt around in the damp hollow to get the lay of the land. But something else was there, too!

I looked into her eyes, surprised. Her answer was a small smile that said I had found her secret. I got on my knees to take a look.

As I parted the hair a ring with a blue gem appeared. My face must have shown my shock.

"It's beautiful," I said of her piercing.

"I've only had it a few months."

"Someone should see this every day, too."

We laughed.

She pulled me back into a kiss.

Finally I pulled away again. "I have to see what it tastes like." I moved lower on her body and started by licking around the ring and lifting it with my tongue. I felt all around it, from one side to the other and back. Her gasping was all I needed. I explored her hole with my fingers as I pulled gently on the ring with my teeth.

Her breathing got heavier. "Oh god!" she screamed.

In answer, I thrust inside while my tongue circled the entire orb and ring. Her legs wrapped around me, and I felt her stiffening. She pulled me closer. My hand went deeper.

My tongue and fingers continued until her entire body tightened around me, shaking us both with its force.

When her breath began to quiet and her muscles relaxed, I disentangled myself and moved up to hold her in my arms.

"Incredible," she gasped, turned toward me, and rested her head against my chest.

That's the way we fell asleep.

It was well after sunrise when I awoke. I could feel her beside me, her breathing soft and peaceful. I looked over at her and took a deep breath. She was beautiful, glowing as she slept. Had I noticed this last night? Sometimes I'm not very observant. I must have, though, or I wouldn't have been there.

I reached over and picked up my clothes from where they'd fallen on the floor. I pulled on my jeans and zipped the fly, then started to button my shirt.

I felt her hand on my thigh.

"Leaving?" she asked as I turned to her.

"I have work to do," I answered as I straightened my socks. I couldn't believe they'd stayed on all night.

"Will I see you again?" The question sounded like a soft request.

"Most definitely." I crawled across the bed and kissed her gently.

Her face erupted into a beautiful smile. Her hand on my face almost stopped me. But I had to leave. If I didn't leave now, I might never.

I slipped into my loafers and let myself out of the apartment. On the street, I realized I was smiling. For the first time in months, I looked forward to the day. I smiled up at the window I calculated was hers and then turned toward the river walk.

As I sauntered away, it hit me. I had never asked her name.

SHAVED

Pascal Scott

Deputy Sheriff Wynonna Fletcher lives in her grandfather's farmhouse at the northernmost edge of Hemphill County, NC. She looks different outside the shooting range in town where we met—more mature, less wild. Or maybe it's the bib apron over her jeans and T-shirt. I've brought a bottle of California Cabernet and a bouquet of summer flowers to our first date. She thanks me, smells the daisies and carnations before putting them in a porcelain vase. She uncorks the wine, starts to pour us both a glass before I can tell her that I don't drink. She offers me sweet tea. Lemonade? Coke? I ask for water, bottled if she has it. She doesn't. Tap is okay, with ice. It's well water, she tells me. That's fine, I say.

"Dinner is just about ready. I'm fixin' barbecued ribs, corn on the cob, and collard greens."

"Let me guess," I say. "Vinegar or ketchup? Umm, you seem like a vinegar girl."

"Hell yeah," she says. "It's a sin to put ketchup on a pig."

"So," I say, sipping my water. "Deputy Sheriff."

She gives me an amused look, as if she's been expecting this.

"Yep."

"How'd that happen?"

She pauses, suddenly more serious.

"I thought I was going to be a nurse," she says. "My first semester at college I was a nursing major."

"Sensible," I say.

"I would have been a good nurse. But then something happened."

She's silent now.

"What happened?" I say, gently.

"I got raped."

"Oh my god, I'm so sorry."

"Yeah, it was date rape, at a fraternity house. One of those situations you get yourself into when you're drinking and not being too smart."

"But it wasn't your fault," I tell her. "Rape is never justified."

"Oh I know that. Now. I know it now. At the time I thought I was to blame. At least partly."

"But you weren't," I assure her. "Did you press charges?"

"No. I just wanted it to go away. I wanted to pretend it never happened."

"It doesn't work that way, does it?"

"No," she says. "It doesn't. So I did what we tell rape victims to do, I got counseling."

"Did that help?"

"It did. I took a semester off and when I came back I changed my major to criminal justice. The department's motto was 'Injustice anywhere is a threat to justice every-where.' It sounds pretty corny but that's what I came to believe."

She clears her throat.

"And the good that came out of it is that Hemphill County has got itself a kick-ass woman Deputy Sheriff now."

"That it has," I say.

She turns back to the pot of greens on the stove, removes the lid, and stirs. I don't know what more to say. I wander into the dining room where a wood-and-glass display case hangs on the wall, filled with antique memorabilia. Her eyes follow me.

"Granddad's," she says.

"Son of the Confederacy," I say, referring to the blazer patch with the Confederate flag.

"Yeah, Granddad was a proud Son. A lot of folks stayed out of the War entirely but the Fletchers served. Where are you from?"

"California, originally. Los Angeles. Born, bred, and fled. I spent a lot of years in the Bay Area."

"I thought you didn't sound like you were from around here."

"My people are. On my mother's side. She was a Thompson. I never knew my father."

"I'm sorry."

"No need. Probably just as well, from what I heard. My mother wasn't much of a fan."

She considers this, starts to say something, and then says something else.

"What was she like?"

"My mother? I don't really know. I only saw her on

Saturdays, for visitation. I grew up in foster care."

"Oh, I'm sorry. That must have been hard."

"Yeah," I say. "It was."

"Is that why you moved to North Carolina? From California? To take care of your mother in her old age?"

"Oh god, no. She died before I moved here. She disowned me when I was twelve. Her lawyer had a hard time finding me, in fact, but he finally did. Thanks to the Internet you can find anybody anymore."

"Her lawyer?"

"Yeah, the estate lawyer. She had actually made a little money in B-movies while she was in Hollywood. I inherited her estate because she died without a will."

"So are you telling me that you're filthy rich?"

"Not rich. Just comfortable."

She thinks about this for a moment.

"Good for you," she says. She seems to mean it.

I change the subject. I look again at the display case.

"So, we have a Son of the Confederacy patch, a ten-dollar Dixie issued by the Confederate State of North Carolina, a certificate of baptism from First Baptist Church, and a Robeson Shuredge razor. Some people might take offense at some of these."

"It's hard for a Yankee to understand. This is something to remember him by. My grandfather was a good man."

"And these are?"

I've wandered back into the kitchen. I'm looking at the photographs on her refrigerator—four redheads with light brown eyes.

"That's me, my sister Ellen, my brother Luke, and Mama."

"And where's Daddy?"

"Out of the picture."

"Literally."

"They're divorced. Mama's living in Dallas with her new husband. Ellen's married with two little girls. They're in Charlotte. And Luke is stationed in Afghanistan."

"Are you close to any of them?"

"I'm close to all of them. Even Daddy. He's got a new wife. They're in Sarasota."

"You're lucky," I say.

There's a photo of Wynonna on her red Sportster, another with a group of Levi and leathered women riders.

"My club," she says. "Tar Heels on Wheels."

"You are something," I say.

She's a good cook, too. I eat everything and ask for a second helping.

"And stop calling me Wynonna. Nobody calls me that. It's Wyn to my friends."

"Wyn," I say. "I like it."

After dinner I help her clear the table. She doesn't have a dishwasher—never put one in—so she fills both sinks with hot water, one soapy, one clear. I grab a towel and dry. We talk about our ancestors landing in Philadelphia, fresh off the boat from Europe, and how they made their way down the Great Wagon Trail to the mountains of North Carolina. It took the Blue Ridge to stop them, the Fletchers and the Thompsons and the rest of the Scots-Irish who emigrated in the eighteenth century. It took a mountain range as old as the earth itself.

While I'm putting up the last of the clean dishes, she pours another glassful of wine. She watches me, sipping, looking me up and down..

"You're very sexy," she says.

"Thank you."

"Not to be rude but—how old are you?"

I have to suppress a smile.

"I turned sixty-two last April."

This stops her short. I watch her expression change.

"Sixty-two," she repeats. "You look younger."

"I get that a lot."

"Sixty-two. Damn."

"How old are you? Not to be rude."

"Forty-two," she answers. "And sixty-two. That's two decades."

"It is," I say.

"Twenty years."

"Do you want me to leave now?"

"No, no, it's just that, well—two decades."

"Listen, if my age is a problem for you, we can stop right now."

She looks at me, her golden-brown eyes a mess of conflicted emotions. Then they settle on one I recognize. She steps forward and takes my hand and leads me to the bedroom. It's been a while since I let a woman undress me. She pulls my shirt over my head, rips my belt out of its loops, unbuttons my 501s. I'm thinking it's true what they say: age is just a number. At least sometimes, when the lights are low and desire has entered the room. As she's pulling off my jeans, she notices the nine-millimeter crater of mottled skin on my left calf.

"What happened here?"

"Yeah that," I say. "That is why I carry a revolver now and not a semiautomatic. I shot myself while I was cleaning my gun."

"You didn't."

"I did. The bullet in the chamber. Famous last words."

Her fingers trace my other scar, the one that's more obvious, the one below my right cheekbone.

"And this?"

"That," I say. "Reformatory. You'd be surprised what those girls can do with a shanked-out toothbrush."

"Reformatory, huh. Do I want to know what you did?"

"No," I say. "You don't."

"Poor baby," she says and pushes me down on the bed and is suddenly on top of me, leaning in for a kiss. I do a quick half sit-up and grab her shoulders, flip her over onto *her* back. I climb on top, straddle her, and just sit there for a moment. Then I lean down, take her arms and pin them over her head, wrist on wrist. I look into her eyes.

"I don't do that," I explain. "I'm always on top."

"Oh," she says. "I didn't know."

I release her arms and let my fingertips slide down her neck, circle one breast and then the other, down to her belly button, and into her nest of pubic hair.

"And while we're talking about sex, I don't do oral unless you shave."

"Oh," she says again.

I stop.

"I have an idea," I say.

In the dining room, I open the glass door of her grandfather's case and remove the Robeson. It's heavier than I would expect, it feels solid in my hand, unlike the razors today. In Wynonna's bathroom I find everything I need: manicure scissors, rubbing alcohol; shaving gel; a washcloth; and a big, soft towel. I notice an electric shaver in the cabinet, for her legs and underarms. *Just in case*, I think. I return to Wynonna in bed with the scissors in my hand.

"Oh lordy," she says.

"You trust me, don't you?"

"I don't really know you," she replies.

"Wrong answer. You trust me, don't you?"

"I guess."

"Wrong again! Third time, you know what they say about charm. You trust me, don't you?"

"Yes, I trust you," she says.

"Good. Now lift up."

I slip the towel under her hips and pull it up as high as her waist. She settles back down.

"Good girl," I say.

"I may regret this," she says.

"Shush now."

The manicure scissors are barely adequate to the task, but I manage to trim her pubic hair until it's short enough for the razor. In the bathroom, I open her grandfather's straight-edge to a four-inch silver steel blade. The handle is bone, off-white in color, and looks like twisted rope. I sanitize the blade with rubbing alcohol. While the straight-edge is air-drying, I let the washcloth warm under hot running water, then I wring it out and take it to bed, where she lies waiting.

"This will feel good," I say.

I untwist the washcloth and spread it over her mound.

"Ummm," she says.

"Told ya. Now you're going to relax and let that do its work."

I look around. There's a CD player on a worn, oak dresser across from the bed.

"Would you like music?"

"Sure," she says. "You pick."

I look through her collection and settle on Claire Mann and Aaron Jones.

"Oh," she says as a Celtic tune begins. "How appropriate."

"Yeah," I agree. "Our kinfolk's music. A fiddle, a flute, and a tin whistle."

I let an instrumental play all the way through before I remove the washcloth and set it on the nightstand. I press the flat of my hand over her pussy. Her hair feels soft and moist.

"Better," I say.

I spray a ben-wa-sized ball of shaving gel onto the tips of my fingers and rub it over the remaining pubic hair, into a whipped-cream-like lather. Her breathing quickens. I spread her legs.

"Don't move."

I retrieve her grandfather's straight-edge. Her eyes widen when she sees it. I lay the blade lightly at the top of her pubes. I ease it down slowly, gently, snowplowing a line until I see perfect, clear skin. I stop dangerously close to her hooded clit. She's holding her breath.

"Breathe," I say, and she does.

I lift the blade, wipe it clean on a section of the towel beneath her, and begin again. I move the blade over slightly, begin at the top of her pubic hair, and slide down; repeat, then reposition and repeat; reposition and repeat until her skin has been shaved clean. I wipe her with the washcloth. There are no bumps, no cuts, not even a nick. I set the straight-edge aside and pick up the electric razor. It starts with a buzz.

"This is for your vulva," I say.

When I'm finished with the electric razor, I turn it off and admire my work.

"Pretty," I say. "That's the front. Now I need you to turn over for me."

"Oh my—"

"Over," I say, more firmly.

She flips over, leaning on her elbows. I slip my hand between her legs and spread her thighs. I use the electric shaver to remove the last of her pubes around her perineum and anus, then wipe her clean with the washcloth.

"Good girl," I say. "Now come with me."

She turns her head to look back at me, puzzled.

"You need to shower off."

I position her to face the shower spray, then rub a washcloth lathered with Dial soap onto her shoulders and down her arms. She's got tats: a heart in memory of Granddad on one shoulder; a cross and John 3:16 on the other; a red Harley on the left cheek of her ass. I turn her around. Water is falling over her face, beading on her skin, she has closed her eyes, and I know this is the scene in the made-for-TV-movie where I am supposed to lean in and kiss her.

Wynonna opens her eyes.

"What's wrong?" she says.

I press my palm into the shaved place between her legs.

"Not a thing," I say.

STRAWBERRY SURPRISE

Anna Watson

Mitzi always said fucking would stop us from growing old, and we went at it like it was a religion. When meno-pause almost took me down—I surely did not feel up to much with all that mess going on—Mitzi's butch diligence got us through. She could walk into the sex store, all silver-fox Daddy, her suit falling just right, shoes shined, and the kids would be lining up to show her the latest products and books for enhancing the mature dyke's sex life. The dick size went down, the quantity of lube went up, but the motion and the emotion remained the same, and I believed her. I believed her when she said we could keep it up forever.

The social worker—her name is the name of a leaf or a tree or something—is one of those straight-up-and-down girls, built like a pencil with a bowl haircut. You could twirl her between your hands and her hair would reach out from her head like an umbrella popping open. We're all in her office: me and Mitzi's kids—the two who like me—and our eldest grandchild, Linda. The third child, the one married to a Tea Party lawyer, we don't have much truck with, and of course she's not here. It's funny how for us it was the butch who came to the relationship with kids, not the femme. I never had any use for men at all, even when I thought I was straight. Queer was what was really going on, although my dad would storm around and call me stubborn, and I could be; I sure could be. "Not stubborn," Mitzi would say when I argued or threw a fit. "That's my *determined* wife."

The kids and the social worker are having a big old confab, and I'm just tuning in and out, but I do hear the words "depression brought on by caretaker fatigue" coming out of that pencil-leaf girl's cavernous mouth. I suppose they're talking about me. I suppose that's what happened to me, the fatigue, because of what happened to Mitzi.

I knew it when I saw her butch wax in the refrigerator instead of on the shelf in the bathroom where she always kept it. Didn't I spend my sixties tending to my own mother when she went gaga? It starts that way, things out of order, because your brain is out of order, and it goes from there. I just knew it, standing there looking at that little jar of hair stuff next to the eggs and half a sandwich from a weekend picnic we'd gone on with the grandkids. I snatched it out and put it back where it belonged. I didn't say anything to Mitzi.

As things got more random in her brain, I did everything I could to help her. Stuck up notes, reminded, shielded her as best I could from her own brain's breakdown. I hated to think about it, and most of the time she was still herself, still my Mitzi. And I came to her in bed; I came to her wearing the slinky underthings she liked, with my cocksucking lipstick painted on and my gray curls loose and falling down my back. Slowly, the harness got to be too much for her, but a consummate cocksman like my husbutch didn't need silicone in order to pleasure her girl.

It got so I couldn't keep Mitzi's condition from her kids anymore, though, and they're the ones who got her the diagnosis. They're the ones who moved us into the assisted living, and I guess it's been okay, even though we're the only queers. I know that my queer ancestors wouldn't have had it this good, even if they'd made it to our age. The staff here mostly treat us like we're married, which we are, and that's even legal. But my Mitzi has left me. They've got her in the "memory neighborhood" now, and I can't believe I can say those words without gagging, those crazy *1984* words, but they trip right off my tongue. "Mitzi is in the memory neighborhood now," I say to our friends at the Council on Aging LGBT events. When I make it out. Which hasn't been lately. I can barely make myself visit my sweet butch who has left me. She left me. She isn't the dear soul I met at the demonstration in 1987, when we were marching on Washington, so many of us! The people, united! We were already in our forties, and Mitzi said we had no time to waste. She fucked me in a hotel bathroom that day, pulled me out of the march and into one of the downtown hotels, bold as you please, queer as you please, and *Up against the wall with you, pretty baby, spread 'em, aren't you the nasty girl with your lacy little panties, wet, too, take them, take my dick fingers, pretty sweet baby.*

It got so I couldn't relax in my apartment in the assisted living, where Mitzi wasn't anymore. I could hear everything in the hall, outside the window. I paced. Linda, our eldest grandchild—queer, too, pied piper, or panpipes or something—she's the one who noticed. "Tatie, you're too skinny"; "Tatie, you haven't been going to meals"; "Tatie, I think something's wrong and I'm taking you to the doctor." I did it for my mother, the taking care of, and now for Mitzi, but I want it to stop. The doctor asked did I want to die? Well, no, of course not. But could it stop?

"Just for a little while," says Linda, when the doctor says she thinks a stay in the geriatric psych ward would be "beneficial." I think of *The Snakepit* and *One Flew Over the Cuckoo's Nest* and the way Big Nurse terrorized the inmates. I'm going to be an inmate. Those freezing cold-water treatments, lobotomies, chemical castration, electric shocks to your brain.

"Stop it, Tatie," says Linda. "They don't do that shit anymore."

I have lost track of time. I don't know how long I've been here. I don't know what day it is when I see a butch by the front desk, rolling up in a wheelchair. She's making choices on the menu for her supper, joshing with Small Nurse. The butch looks like she has her faculties about her. She looks like she has a hearty appetite. I'd been sitting with my roommate, Queen of All She Surveys. I like the way Queen bosses everyone around, since I can barely manage to ask for soap so I can take a shower, but she's not very good company. Always complaining. Linda had called and said she couldn't visit that evening, and I know I can't expect her to leave her busy life all the time and come see me every day, I know that. I miss her. I miss Mitzi, but even if she were right here with me, she wouldn't be.

She hasn't quite forgotten how to eat yet, but other things. Most things. Me.

The butch in the wheelchair finishes her order and hands the menu over to Small Nurse with a flourish. She's heavyset, wearing her own bathrobe, fuzzy fleece with pictures of hunting dogs on it. Her feet are swaddled in the bright yellow non-slip loony-bin socks we all have to wear, but I bet she has leather scuffs at home. Head shaved except for a quiff right at the front, dyed a bright pinky-red.

"Oh, that's a nice color!" says Pencil-Leaf, galumphing down the corridor on her lanky legs.

"Tell her what it's called," says Small Nurse in that voice they all use.

The butch sees me looking and leans back in her wheelchair. "Strawberry Surprise," she says, winking at me.

"That's so cute!" coos Pencil-Leaf, in that voice. I don't think the butch is listening to her, though. I think the butch is watching me blush instead.

People usually let me sit by myself in the rec room, over at the farthest table, the one looking out on Memorial Drive. The cars just go and go and go. All those people out there, going along.

"Well, they told me to get out of my room and socialize," someone says, a gravelly voice, the kind of voice I know and love. She bellies up to the table in her wheelchair, maneuvering herself so that her knee is almost touching mine.

I'm not wearing lipstick. I forgot it and then forgot to ask Linda to bring me any.

"Well, I don't know how social I'm going to be," I say, trying for flirtatious but ending up with whiney. "Broken down old me."

"Peas in a pod," she says, lifting her eyebrows. "My head is murky with all the crap drugs they gave me."

"It gets me in the stomach," I say, nodding. She's looking at me so strong. That gaze. Mitzi had it, and then it dimmed and died. I could be anyone when I go to visit her. I want to ask the butch what's wrong with her, if it's serious, if she's crazy, but we don't ask each other things like that in here. Instead, I ask her if she has a roommate.

"No, but I live in fear."

I want to laugh but all I can do is twitch up one side of my mouth. Still, something is happening. Something is tapping on my heart, bubbling in my bloodstream. "You're lucky. Mine is over there. The Queen of All She Surveys."

The butch snorts and turns around to see who I'm talking about. The Queen is laughing and talking loudly to two newbies. She is much admired for the luster of her hair and her fashion sense. Suddenly, I don't want the butch to look at her too hard. I touch her on her knee. That bathrobe is fuzzy and her knee is warm and solid underneath.

"She wears those things, those Depends," I say, and then I regret my unkindness, and what if the butch has to wear them, too? It happens. But she's back looking right at me, and she snorts again. "Poor thing," she says. And "Meow!"

"I'm sorry!" Now both sides of my mouth have twitched up.

"No, don't be. Anything to keep sane in here, am I right? And don't worry—it's quite clear that your hair is prettier and your outfit is better, too."

How can that be? I'm wearing nothing, nothing of any consequence, a blouse, some slacks, a far cry from the funky artsy garb I'd affected in my maturity, the pashminas, the flowing skirts. And I've gotten so damn skinny!

"Tatiana," I say, reaching out my hand. "Tatie."

"A beautiful, old-world name," she says, taking my hand in both of hers. "I'm Phil."

The next day and the next we sit together in the rec room after the news group and the singing group and the OT. That bubbling around my heart gets stronger. What am I doing here? I've been asking myself that more and more. Linda had to go on a trip for work; the others come for short little visits, obviously wishing they didn't have to. It's okay. People come and go on the ward, but so far, Phil is still with us. I look for her every morning. She has cranberry juice for breakfast and an egg over easy. Marble rye toast. Grape jelly. She got a roommate and now she tells me funny stories in a whisper about the things the poor gal says in her sleep.

One afternoon the old loudmouth retired Episcopal priest lets his bathrobe flop open and out flops his wrinkly old dong. Phil makes her snort, but quietly, because the other ladies are so distressed, and Big and Small Nurses get him out of there but quick. No dongs allowed in the rec room, but no one can stop me from looking at Phil's big hands as she rests them on her lap. There's a pale strip of skin around her pinky finger—no rings allowed in here, either—and that pale band matches the pale strip of skin around my left ring finger. She shoots the cuffs of her bathrobe and I can see her faded blue star. Mitzi never did, but a lot of the butches used to have them, covered by their watches during the day when they were at work. I haven't seen one in so long. I shut my eyes on the afterimage of that old star.

It's evening and we're waiting for our meds. It just seems to take forever. The headlights of all those cars out on Memorial Drive are so bright. I look away to where Phil is sitting next to me, closer than she was the last time I looked. Our knees almost touching, the way we like. I can't help it, the big question pops out of my mouth, "What am I doing here?" and Phil's eyes light up. She beckons, and I lean in. Her voice is low so no one can hear.

"What are you doing here?" she repeats. "I know what you're doing here, Tatie. You're here because here is where we meet. Here is where we find each other. Here is where it all begins." She takes my hand and turns it over, cradling it. She places her raspy fingertips on the inside of my wrist like she's feeling for my pulse. "You've been keeping yourself sweet for me, haven't you?"

Does she mean that I got Linda to bring me lipstick and my red-and-black pashmina? My leggings with the shooting stars on them and my black silky blouse? Does she somehow know that for the past two nights I've been sucking my fingers until they're wet and dancing circles on my clit until I come and come again, always quiet, never making any noise, timing it between the nurse's rounds? "I have been," I whisper back, nodding. I let a lock of my crazy-curly hair fall across the side of my face; all those gray curls: Mitzi used to tangle her fingers up in them and gently tug. Phil reaches out and brushes the curls away so she can see my eyes. When she strokes the side of my face, I shiver to my core. I feel myself breaking out in goose bumps.

"I knew it," says Phil, stroking me some more. "I knew you were a feeling girl, an easy girl. Come more than once, don't you, Tatie? Don't you? Fast and easy and sweet for me?"

How does she know? One night, Mitzi and I just stopped counting. "You're going to kill me!" I squealed, panting and laughing and squirming around on the bed, covers all over the room, who knew what time in the wee hours it had gotten to be.

"Going out in a blaze of glory," she growled before getting back to work with her mouth. Each time a surprise, a gift. "You are a marvel," said Mitzi, no, it's Phil saying it. "You are a marvel and you are here with me."

There's nowhere for us to go to be alone. She passes me in the hall and she whispers, "You'll ride my cock." Big Nurse, walking beside me—does she hear? Her poochy cheeks keep up their rhythmic motion without stopping; she's always chewing gum.

Phil and I sit together at supper and she holds up her knife, just a plastic thing because loony-bin inmates don't get to have real metal silverware. She holds it up, waggles it slightly, her tongue poking out just a bit, and I know what she means. I lick my lips, red with cocksucking lipstick, wet with want.

She scribbles a note on a scrap of paper as we sit in group, the one where we have to fill in crossword puzzles together, the OT providing us with the first letter of each word. Phil's note says, *Rhymes with a common water fowl; what will happen for approximately a full day and night once we're sprung and I get you to my place.*

When the service dog comes in, a sweet chocolate lab named Blossom, Phil rolls up beside me, her hand finding mine as we rub Blossom's round tummy as she lies flat on her back with her legs splayed, tail wagging. Phil grasps me hard on the skin between thumb and finger, pulls, then slots her fingers there and squeezes. It's over in a flash, but I feel it. *Nothing wrong with your brain,* said Mop-Head earlier this week. *Sad and tired and old,* I said, but it turns out there isn't anything wrong with my cunt, either, because it gets the message from Phil's strong fingers and sends me a jolt. I gasp and Blossom turns her head, looking at me with concern, then flops back down with a sigh when Phil and I burst into laughter.

I wish she could come to my bed. The Queen snores and I wet down my fingers.

She's gone the day after Blossom visits. We'd known she was getting out, but I hadn't expected her to leave so early. Small Nurse sees me searching, and shuffles over to give me a piece of paper.

Phyllis asked me to give this to you," she says. That voice. "How nice that you made a friend!" She all but pats me on the head, then shuffles off.

I go into the rec room and sit watching the cars on Mem Drive for a while with the paper in my lap. It has a weight, a heat. Finally, I open it. *Where I am and where you'll be.* Already, I recognize her handwriting, the sloppy open *A*s, the spiky *W*s. An address in Somerville—I'll have to take the bus, am I going to be able to take the bus? Yes. Of course. Then four boxes, like a crossword puzzle, the first letter filled in: *F.* I look over at Small Nurse, who must have read this, but she's not even watching. "Flying under the radar," Phil had said a few days earlier, copping a quick feel of my thigh under the table, no tablecloth or anything to hide us, if anyone had been watching. Do they have a policy about fraternization like a dorm or a barracks? "Right under the radar." Phil put her hand higher, cupping the crease of my thigh, then my pussy so briefly, so sweetly. No one noticed, or if they did, it was only the Queen, who had her own affairs to tend to.

That evening, Linda is in the dining room when I get out of group.

"Look, Tatie!" she says, standing to hug me. "The first strawberries!" They're slightly squashed from riding in her bike bag, jumbled together in their little wooden container, the thin slats stained with red. I can smell them.

"Oh, Linda, they're gorgeous! Thank you!"

"You're welcome, Tatie! Fuck, it's good to see you smile!" I smile even wider, making a grab for the berries. It's not very polite, with a couple of other inmates watching enviously, and the berries probably aren't even washed, but I can't wait any longer. I snatch up a handful and press them into my mouth.

The warmth of the sun. The smell of freshly plowed earth. The feeling of a cool little breeze caressing the back of your sweaty neck on a hot, hot afternoon. I close my eyes and throw my head back. "Mmm!"

Linda starts to laugh. "Tatie, you look like you're going to come!" she hisses.

The Queen of All She Surveys glides up. "May I?" Her hand hovers over the basket.

"Of course." I'm going home in three days, and I heard Small Nurse saying the Queen has at least another two weeks. I push the basket over to her, full of the loveliest things to have been in the dining room for as long as we've been there. "Please, take as many as you'd like."

We finish the basket in short order and that night, when I lick my fingers to get them good and wet, they still taste like strawberries.

CINEMA FANTASTIQUE

Victoria Janssen

The old Mackenzie Theater downtown was an utter dump. In its heyday, the 1940s, it had been lauded as a palace of cinema, but by the time Sunshine Jackson was a teenager in the 1970s, the green-velvet seat covers were worn bare in spots, and the swathes of faded green-and-gold curtain reeked of dust, mildew, weed, and cigarettes. Evening shows cost a dollar, the afternoon matinee was fifty cents, and the popcorn was always stale. The Mackenzie was the most popular date venue in town, not because of its historic charm but because there was a balcony, and the balcony seats were cushioned pews instead of armchairs. If you didn't mind company a short distance away, those pews were much better for fucking than the backseat of even the most capacious LTD, especially in winter. Or so the gossip said.

In high school, Sunshine and her pack of five friends went in a herd to the Mackenzie almost every week, to the cheap matinees, critiquing action flicks while sneaking joints. Occasionally they would deign to cast disparaging glances at the paired-up older kids, who would head for the balcony without a second glance. Her pack was half girls and half boys, but they weren't *together*. They were above that, plus Sunshine liked that nobody could tell she was more into girls than boys, even though she wasn't with any of them. No matter how cute Amie Itzkoff happened to be, with her skinny yet graceful body and tiny round glasses and plaid ties. The pack went for the movies, not the sleazy groping. Or at least, that's what they pretended. It was good to have a pack, to never have to wonder what you were going to do on a Friday night, or with whom.

The pack saw *Star Wars* at the Mackenzie eighteen times in total; twice on some days. They memorized lines and quoted them to each other like their own private code. Sunshine wanted to be Han Solo, only with tits. If she wished, in her secret heart, that Amie would invite her into the balcony, she reminded herself that Han Solo ought to be the one asking, and would get dressed for the movie hoping her black vest or her tall boots would lend her mercenary-pilot bravado. But she never quite had the courage to ask, in the end, because she wasn't Han Solo; she just wished to be. And she'd feared what would happen if Amie said no, and feared even more what would happen if Amie said yes.

Sunshine left her whole hometown behind, including Amie, when she went to Oberlin, but she kept the Mackenzie. The grimy balcony lurked in her subconscious for decades. She and Francine, her first girlfriend in college, went to an Italian art film on their third date, and she was painfully disappointed when the modern theater turned out to be balcony-less. It was just a movie, just a room where movies were shown, and it smelled only of popcorn and sugar, not cigarettes and mildew.

The Mackenzie emerged unexpectedly in her dreams, her daydreams, and her fantasies for years; it took up permanent residence in the sexual halls of her mind. The most forbidden fantasy, which she only let herself have a few times, was of her and Amie, still back in high school, sneaking up just before the rebels set out in their X-Wings to destroy the Death Star. She always felt a little depressed after she'd indulged in that one. She'd lost touch with Amie after *The Empire Strikes Back* came out, because Amie had gone out to California for college, and Sunshine never found out what Amie thought of *Return of the Jedi*. She had let it happen, even though they'd both eventually gone into architecture at graduate schools separated by a thousand miles. She never even knew for sure if Amie liked girls. Amie had never had a boyfriend in high school, but then, neither had any of the girls in their pack. Two of the other three were married now, both to men, and one had transitioned to male and moved to Des Moines.

If Amie had married a man, Sunshine didn't want to know.

Then one day, her cell rang. She didn't recognize the number. "Hello?"

"Sunshine?"

She knew the voice immediately. They exchanged quick histories of recent years. Amie had spent time in Chicago before she moved back to their hometown when she learned of plans to revive the main street and several of the historic businesses. There was a sizable grant to support the work, and she was putting in two more applications. "There's an incredible amount to do, Sunshine, but I think it's a terrific project. I always loved all the old buildings in town when I was a kid, and it was a real heartbreaker to see some of them with collapsing ceilings and basement leakage."

"Did the theater ceiling collapse? That painted ceiling?"

"No, it's still intact, though the paint's flaking, especially in the corners. I was in on the inspection for that. I never realized before how much the mural figures had been darkened from dirt and smoke. They were naked! Just imagine if we'd known about that in high school."

Sunshine cradled her phone closer to her face. "I knew. My granny told me. She thought they were scandalous. But I think my mom might have been conceived there, so . . . "

Amie laughed. "Maybe that's why no one bothered to clean them up before this—keep down population growth. But ceiling art restoration is way in the future. What I'd like you to do is inspect the interiors. We can put that together with the reports we already have on the facade and the overall structural integrity—I can email those to you. Oh, and I especially want you to have a look up in the balcony. You remember what it used to look like, don't you? I never went up there back in the day, not once." Amie paused. Sunshine could sense her wanting to ask, and hesitating.

Sunshine changed the subject. It was easy. They'd always had a lot to talk about. It turned out Amie had loathed the Ewoks in *Return of the Jedi*, and lacked confidence in the longevity of Leia and Han's relationship.

They rang off with a promise they'd go out to dinner when Sunshine arrived in town. They'd meet up at a new restaurant on Main Street, a Thai place neither of them could have imagined when they were in high school.

Amie wasn't married. Amie was single. Amie now knew that Sunshine wasn't straight.

Sunshine bought a plane ticket before the week was out.

Walking into the Mackenzie in the summer of 2016 was like falling into a swamp of memories. A steamy swamp, as the ancient, cobbled-together air-conditioning had failed about a decade earlier. Sunshine left her roll-away suitcase just inside the green double doors opening from the lobby. The old familiar fug of ancient cigarettes and mildew invaded her nose and soaked into her clothes as she climbed ladders and scrambled over piles of old construction trash, tapping out notes on the details of the building's features and their current state. Dust glued itself to her sweaty bare legs and arms. She felt like an archaeologist, and briefly entertained images of herself in an Indiana Jones–style fedora.

Then it was time for the balcony.

Climbing the narrow stairs made her feel weak in the knees. She took a couple of swigs from her water bottle; it was ridiculously hot in here, and she was probably dehydrated, though her hands were sweaty on her tablet and her camera strap stuck to her neck. She laid her tablet on one of the long pews and began taking photographs. Lost in her work, she startled violently when someone shouted her name from down below.

She leaned over the plaster-embellished railing and saw familiar carroty hair below. It was cropped very short now, very butch. Amie apparently couldn't wait until dinner tonight. "Up here," Sunshine said.

Amie had grown taller since Sunshine had last seen

her, or maybe it was her dinged-up cowboy boots; gold caps adorned the pointed toes. She wore an ancient pair of Levi's that clung to her slender thighs and a sleeveless cotton button-up in an orange plaid that clashed with her hair. Sunshine didn't care. Amie was grinning at her, and when Amie hugged her she felt solid strength all down her front. Sunshine's fingers fisted in Amie's shirt, gripping her muscled shoulders, before she remembered how sweaty and filthy she was. "Agh! Your shirt! Sorry!"

Amie gave her one last squeeze, leaned in, and kissed her forehead. "You are more beautiful than I ever imagined you could become."

That answered one question.

"I know," Sunshine said, and grinned. Amie caught the reference to Han and Leia without losing a beat, and they both laughed. "Here, have a look at my photos."

They sat closely together on one of the pews, legs touching despite the close heat. That answered another question.

Amie's arm brushed Sunshine's arm or her chest while hitting the camera controls, flipping back to something she'd missed. It was like when they'd shared *X-Men* comics from the drugstore when they were kids, and Sunshine couldn't stop smiling. But it also wasn't like sharing comics, because the slick heat between her legs wasn't all sweat.

"I bet you're wondering why I showed up here instead of at the restaurant tonight," Amie said at last, and brushed Sunshine's shoulder. "Cobweb," she said. Her eyes were locked on Sunshine's, her breathing faster than before.

Sunshine didn't say anything, because she wasn't

wondering. She lifted her camera strap over her head and hung it from the end of the pew. Then she cupped Amie's face in her hands and kissed her.

The sound Amie made was delicious, sending a dizzy bolt through her. Amie's arms went around her; long-fingered hands slid up Sunshine's back, mirroring the slide of a tongue in her mouth. Sunshine gripped Amie's head more firmly, craving smooth skin against her aching palms.

One of Amie's hands crept around to cup her breast. Sunshine said, "Yes," and set to work nibbling Amie's earlobe and stroking her fingers through Amie's soft fuzz of hair. After a while, she took Amie's hand and slipped it beneath her shirt. She sighed when Amie opened her blouse, flicked her bra open, and teased her nipple until she felt as if she would dissolve into a pool of desire.

The balcony was hot and dusty and dark. She could smell her own sweat and desire, could smell Amie in the soft skin behind her ear.

"Yes, yes," she murmured, as she was pushed back onto the pew. It was narrow and hard, the velvet cushions long since disintegrated. Amie stretched out over her, one of her feet braced on the floor. Her cowboy boot thumped against the splintery wood as she shifted position, trying to squeeze closer.

"This is so much better than I ever imagined," Amie said in her ear, before bending down to suck her nipples, switching from one to the other as if she couldn't decide which she liked better.

Sweet hard thigh muscles pressed through denim, pushing hard against Sunshine's cunt. She slid her hands under Amie's shirt, nails lightly scratching.

Amie groaned and rubbed against her leg. Muffled by

breasts, she said, "I want you so much, but it's so nasty up here." She stamped her heel on the floor. "I think I stepped in some prehistoric gum."

Sunshine laughed, holding Amie to her so they wouldn't fall onto the dirty floor. Amie grabbed the back of the pew. They rocked together, unsteadily, and that was sexy, too, their breasts smashing together and their hips bumping. Sunshine wriggled experimentally. Amie gasped. "The filth wasn't part of my fantasy, either," she said. "There was never any mess. We always just shared glorious orgasms just before I fell asleep. But I don't want to stop now. I've—"

"—been waiting a long time for this." Amie leaned her face close to Sunshine's, so close that vision smeared and there was nothing to do but open her mouth to draw in Amie's scent and then her breath.

Amie had to scramble to her feet to get her jeans and underwear unfastened and shoved down. Sunshine grinned as she watched, and then delicately lifted the hem of her flowy short skirt and tossed it over her belly. Her bikini underwear displayed Darth Vader's helmet, right over her mound.

"I want those," Amie said, in tones of deepest desire. She knelt beside the pew, her jeans protecting her knees, and buried her face in Darth Vader, breathing out hot moist breath and curling her fingers under the thin black waistband, slowly tugging down. She had to stop twice to giggle like a maniac.

Sunshine's fantasies had never gone this far. This was better than any movie. She writhed beneath Amie's tongue and the hard press of teeth behind her lips. She gripped the smooth back of the pew with one hand and cupped Amie's shorn head with the other. "Touch yourself," she said.

"Oh fuck," Amie said. She eased a finger into Sunshine, teasing her clit with her thumb, and then began to tease herself left-handed. "Do you like what I'm doing to you? What I'm doing to me? The whole theater down there knows. They know why we came up here. They know why we came up here together."

"I know. I want them to know. I want you. I want them to know I want you. I wanted . . . but I couldn't . . . "

"I know, Sunny. I know. Me, too, though it took me a while to figure it out."

Sunshine wasn't sure how long they worked together in the hot darkness. Amie had to shift position on the hard floor more than once, and Sunshine crooked her leg over Amie's shoulder while Amie worked at her with both fingers and mouth, her other hand teasing herself with increasing intensity.

Amie's second finger, inside Sunshine, curled up to meet her thumb's intense pressure. Sunshine squeezed around her hand, clenching every muscle as she strained for her peak, gasping out Amie's name when she came.

Amie withdrew her hand and eased Sunshine down gently with lips and tongue. Drowsily, Sunshine asked, "You?"

"Oh, hell yes." Amie shifted position, splaying herself open so Sunshine could watch; Sunshine reached out and fondled one of Amie's nipples as she brought herself off, silent and intense, her skin flushed from cheeks to chest.

"Next time, I want to make you scream," Sunshine murmured, stroking Amie's cropped hair. Because there would be a next time.

At last they stood and put their clothes in order.

Sunshine turned around and Amie brushed at her shirt, with what seemed to be a futile effort, if Sunshine could go by the sounds she was making. "Don't tell me what's on me," Sunshine pleaded. "I have clean clothes in my bag downstairs."

Amie said, "About future glorious orgasms. At home, I built a glorious rainstorm shower. And I have a bed. A very nice bed in an alcove with no dust, dried mildew, or cobwebs."

Sunshine wrapped her arms around Amie's waist and they hugged in silence for long moments, sweat and grime and all. "Yes, yes, yes."

Amie groaned. "So, can we move on to the showering-together fantasy I've been having since I installed the new fixtures? The future orgasms could happen then. And then making love in my bed? And then, maybe talking about how long you can stay around?"

Sunshine grinned and kissed her collarbone. "I think I would be into that."

ORIGINS

Amanda Rodriguez

Nowadays everybody knows who I am. I seep into the edges of conversation. I'm in regular rotation on the nightly news. Folks think they know my story because of that first big hoopla I made in the papers when I ended that standoff at the bank, but someone discovered me long before that. That's when I became something. My story begins on that night.

I was in a club, feeling nothing but the bass in my bones and the sway of my limbs. When I closed my eyes, the flash of strobe lights illuminated my darkened lids. When I opened them again, a woman was staring at me with one side of her mouth hooked into a wry smile. She was tall with evocative curves and big, black eyes. I casually danced closer, only glancing at her once in a while, trying to play it cool. Every time I looked at her, she was looking back at me. She wasn't shy. Maybe I shouldn't be either.

I walked over close and stood looking up into her eyes. She began to dance around me, not touching me, sensuously moving her long body like a snake. Then she ran one light-brown finger down my dark-brown chest, tracing a line of sweat that ran between my breasts. The world receded as her finger lingered on me. As if hypnotized, I let her take my hands and put them on her. Together we moved. The beat infused our movements with rapture. Our wet limbs entwined like water. Our hips thrummed with fire.

Some guy came up behind me and put his hands on my ass. The steamy, sexy spell was broken. Outrage choked me. I slapped him away, yelling, "Fuck off, creep!" My fingers spasmed.

He moved behind my dance partner and pawed at her. She swatted at him like the cockroach he was.

Then it happened . . . again. My vision blurred as my eyes rattled around in their sockets. All the hairs on my body stood up, and gooseflesh rushed to cover every inch of my skin. My teeth tattooed a spastic rhythm. The ground shook, and the concrete floor cracked in a circle beneath my feet.

I reached a shaking hand out to the man harassing her and grabbed his wrist. He stopped kneading her thigh and went rigid. His eyes rolled back, and he convulsed. I dropped his wrist, afraid of what I'd done.

All the manic energy drained from me, and my vision cleared. The woman blinked from me to him, her mouth a shocked O. I shrunk into myself, turned and pushed to the exit. The air in that place was too hot and too close.

When I spilled into the street, the night was cool with a light, misting rain. Bent double, I swallowed deep breaths and whoa'ed my heart to slow its canter. I looked up to see her standing in front of me.

"Holy shit," she said, her voice a higher pitch than I'd expected. "What did you do to him?"

I could only dully shake my head.

"That was so fucking cool!" Was that awe in her voice? Reverence? My eyebrows drew together. She grabbed my hand and pulled me into a run.

"C'mon! Let's get out of here before that asshole recovers or the po-po show!"

With her warm hand enveloping mine, it was hard to focus on the thoughts ricocheting like bullets in a barrel around my brain. I picked up my pace until our strides slapped the damp pavement like matched heartbeats.

Between puffs of breath that clouded the cold air, I asked, "Where are you taking me?"

She flashed a wide, red-lipped, Cheshire-cat grin. "Patience, my dear!"

For the next few blocks, all I could think about was that mouth, that mouth, that *mouth*. I was still imagining how acrobatic a mouth that big must be when she abruptly stopped.

We stood in front of Cat's Corner, a greasy spoon diner. The large windows were smudged with grease and fingerprints. The booths looked like an ancient mountain lion with blunted claws used them for scratching posts. The people inside moved lethargically as if the air had heft to it.

I arched a brow. "Is this the place you take all your potential conquests?"

"Only the superhuman ones who might be on the lam from the law."

I flinched.

"Plus, they have the *best* fries."

I squared my shoulders. "I will judge them by their milkshakes."

We were seated at a two-top booth that was so small our knees touched beneath the table. Her hands rested in her lap, and her fingertips brushed my leg. My esteem for the place rose.

I gave her an appraising look, which she returned. Thankfully, half the lights in the place were busted, so we weren't bathed in unflattering fluorescent spotlights. Her olive skin was shiny from the rain. She had bold, liquid eyes that matched her confident mouth. After our run, the fine, dark hair piled on top of her head was an artful mess. A head and a half taller than me, she had curves for days.

I hoped I passed muster with my compact form, shaggy hair, and deep-brown skin.

Her glistening fries arrived along with my enormous strawberry milkshake. Feeling oddly exposed, I slurped down a couple of quick swallows of shake.

"Wow," I said. "I think they use real, actual strawberries."

She snatched her hands away from the fries, shaking burnt fingers. "Never judge a diner by its"—she looked around us—"everything."

"So who are you, mystery lady?"

There was that wry smile again. Her words came fast. "I'm Amira. I was born in Pakistan, but my parents moved to the States when I was four. I'm a programmer at a tech firm. Snore. I've lived in a loft a couple blocks from here for six or seven years. And my cat, Witchy, is the boss of me."

I closed one eye and squinted out the other one. "Tell me something sexy about you."

She leaned in closer, her round, braless breasts resting on the table. "What *isn't* sexy about me?"

I wondered what it would feel like to hold each of her breasts in my hands. How heavy would they be? Would her nipples grow hard under my thumbs? What sound would she make if I touched those nipples with my breath? Grazed them with my lips?

Her smile quirked at me. "I like to play video games in lingerie." Without missing a beat, she continued, "But I think the real question is 'what's *your* name?'"

"Mora," I said. "It means blackberry in Spanish. My parents always say I was sweet and dark as a blackberry when I was born."

"Are you sure it's not Quake? She-Shake? Maybe The Southern Rattler? Maybe you're a member of a superhero club?"

I looked down at my melting pink shake. My hair fell into my eyes. "No one's ever seen me do that before . . . or more like no one's ever known it was me who was doing it before. It's like you're the only one who's ever really *seen me*."

I dared to look up at her from behind my bangs. Her eyes were round, her lashes a painter's elegant feathered brushstrokes. "How?" she asked. "When I saw you back there, you were a magnetic pulse that I could feel through all the noise. Like a desert calling to water, I felt you calling to me."

My lips parted, and I let loose a whisper of a gasp.

She flashed a fox grin. "Plus, girl, you are a whole lot of hotness in such a small package." She put on a twang,

"And that down South accent, mmm. I could just eat . . . you . . . up . . . ."

I snorted. She reached across the table and gripped my arms. Her touch sent waves of heat through my body, making me question which one of us had superpowers.

"Seriously, you've got to tell me. I'll die of the shame of ignorance if you don't. Literally. I'll die a hot, lonely tech nerd. You'll have basically killed the digital age equivalent of a sexy librarian."

Thinking, I licked my lips. "Invite me back to your place, and I'll tell you everything."

Like a withering flower, she drew back her outstretched arms. "Is it . . . I don't know . . . safe? You've got some serious, uh, kick when you get worked up."

She was right; it probably wasn't safe, but my heart was hammering out a syncopated ditty. My thoughts were clouded with the sweet scent of her. I ached with want and had to squirm in my seat.

In the quiet fields of North Carolina where I'd grown up, I had practiced controlling my power on broken tables and rusted-out cars. In the secret of solitude, I'd even used that power on myself, regulating the waves of vibration for pleasure and, sometimes, a delicious edge of pain.

Mustering a veneer of confidence, I said, "Take me to bed and find out."

By the time we left the diner, the sky had let loose its troubles. We flat-out ran for Amira's apartment while the fat raindrops soaked us through. Her hand clasped mine and practically dragged me up the flights of stairs. Before I could settle my breathing, we were inside her apartment.

She made no move to turn on a light. Instead she let me stand there, looking around. Her place had big windows.

The city lights shone through, casting abstract shadows across our faces. I fumbled with a floor lamp until a feeble, amber light emerged from its Edison bulb. The apartment was one open room, and my eyes lingered on the neatly made bed. The floor was old, scarred wood. Little toys sat like totems in twos and threes on the mantle, coffee table, and counter. I recognized a *Legend of Zelda* figurine and smiled.

Then I looked at her. In the soft light, her face was anxious. Almost against my will, my gaze was drawn downward. The wet fabric of her pale dress clung to her curves. I could see her dark nipples and the outline of her thighs through the thin fabric. The dress cleaved to the place where her legs met. I stepped toward her, reaching. I stopped in mid-motion, my arms halfway extended.

I swallowed. "Is it okay if I kiss you?"

Amira didn't say anything.

I whispered, "Ever since I saw you, I've wanted to touch you. Can I?"

She bit her lip, weighing, deciding, choosing.

Then her lips were on me; her body against mine. If I was the quavering earth, she was fire made flesh. Her skin steamed beneath her wet clothes, and her big mouth enveloped me. She swallowed me, consumed me. My universe was her mouth, her lips, her tongue. Our breath was a living being, passing back and forth between us. She nipped me, and the flash of pain was exquisite, lighting up my body, reminding me I *had* a body. I had been born with hands to worship at the altar of her.

I drew my hands up her legs, pulling her dress up over her head. I stood transfixed, staring at the mound of her hip and curve of her breasts, each nipple like an upturned purple bud seeking sunlight. She tore off my shirt and unzipped my pants. I knelt before her, tracing the line of her little red panties with the tip of my tongue. Her hands in my hair, she moaned and leaned into me.

With agonizing slowness, I used only my teeth to tug her panties down. Small gasps kept escaping her. I wanted to bury my face between her legs and lap like a kitten at her clit, but I held back. Instead I darted my tongue out in quick motions, licking the lips that were hidden beneath soft, black hair. My darting tongue parted those lips, but I wasn't ready yet to search for her treasures.

"You tease, Mora," she moaned.

I laughed and stood up. "I can't have you coming too quick, sugar."

We kissed and petted each other, laughing and stumbling to Amira's bed. She was on top of me, towering over me like a goddess. Her hand snaked down my pants. When her fingertips found my clit, it was like an electric jolt ran through me, and I cried out and spread my legs wider, my body, of its own will, begging for more.

She bit my ear and growled, "You're *so* wet."

Soon I was bucking against her hand, gliding up and down the lengths of her fingers. Two fingers slid inside me for an instant, and then they were gone, back to their rapid, slippery strokes. Her mouth was on my nipple. She bit and sucked and caressed it.

"You have the perkiest little tits," she breathed.

"Please." I begged, not knowing what for.

Her fingers were back inside me, and I ground my pelvis against them. I threw my head back, panting. Then her fingers were outside me again, rubbing my clit in circles until I ached with the need for release. Suddenly a torrent of heat and pleasure wracked me, and I was calling out her name.

I lay there, catching my breath.

She said, "My philosophy is cum early and cum often."

I laughed. "Touché."

I kissed her then like kissing was the only language I knew. My eyes were closed, but every part of her I touched came into sharp focus. The supple skin of her belly beaded with sweat. The delicate hairs on her arms standing on end as she shivered beneath my touch. The strength of her long legs as they gripped me. She was the only thing real in this world, the only person to truly know me and to trust me. I'd been with other women, but I had always kept the truth of me secret. Over the years, this power of mine had become my weakness. Her desire for me in spite of, or maybe because of, that power was a gift, and I intended to show my gratitude.

My touch light as a breath, I ran my hand down her chest, down her belly, to rest on the pulsing lips between her legs. Her hips thrust forward, but I kept my touch gentle. My fingertips probed, seeking the heart of her. I wanted to lay eyes on her hard, beautiful clit, but for now I would have to content myself with imagination. With the greatest care, I let my fingertips minutely thrum.

She gasped in shock. In the next breath, she laughed.

"You're amazing," she said.

"I'm just getting started," I murmured.

"Mmm," she cooed. "Giddyup."

Like a radio frequency, I tuned in to her. Listening, feeling, gauging what would make her sing to me. Her body was an exquisite violin, and I the lowly violinist who sought to release her innate music. She writhed and panted as if in a trance. I was in awe of her beauty.

I turned the intensity of the vibrations up and up, searching beyond what she wanted for what she *needed*. My hand blurred with steady speed. She gripped the sheet in her fist. Her teeth bit into my shoulder, muffling the cry that exploded from her as she convulsed in climax.

Before she could recover, I pulled her on top of me, my fingers slipping inside her. I paired the vibrations with the slow beckoning motion of my fingers. With my free hand, I kneaded the generous flesh of her ass. Like a queen, Amira sat tall atop me. Her broad, dark shoulders and full breasts filled my vision. Her hips rocked in time with my movements.

I spread undulations outward to my palm and then pressed it against her clit. As her excitement increased, her rocking became more forceful. She rode me hard and fast. Her bobbing breasts mesmerized me. I squeezed one of those breasts, rubbing and pinching her nipple.

"I love watching you," I said.

Her hair was loose and wild across her face. She looked at me through slit cat eyes. Then she bent forward to kiss me, the whole of her naked torso against me.

We grappled and rolled until I was once again on top of her.

"Mora . . . Mora, *mi amor,*" she purred.

Through the glaze of my desire, I looked up at her. "*¿Tu hablas español?*"

She shook her head, for the first time almost shy. "But you can speak it to me."

So I did. My words were muffled with mouthfuls of her, but I crooned to her in my milk tongue. It was freeing for her not to understand my words. I swung between pillow talk that I'd be ashamed to say in a language she knew and my deepest, unspoken truths.

I couldn't resist any longer. I slid down her long body and nuzzled between her legs. I savored the velvety feel of her and the sharp, honeyed taste of her. My tongue ran her length, discovering her soft, secret places. Amira was languorous and accepting of my exploring licks and caresses.

I pressed the flat of my pulsing tongue against her. Again, she gasped, but this time the gasp trailed off into a moan as she ground herself against my face. Greedy for more, she cupped the back of my neck and drew me even closer. As I upped the intensity, her hands left my neck and clutched the headboard above her. I reached up and stroked one of her breasts. With the other hand, I buried my vibrating fingers deep inside her. Like I was the holy woman and she the possessed, Amira's body flew up off the bed. My tongue and fingers trembled. I sucked and licked until she screamed. I drew the orgasm out of her like a living thing.

She glowed with sweat, and her chest heaved. I crawled back up her, dropping gentle kisses as I went.

"Wow," she said. Her voice was hoarse. "How many girls did you have to practice on to perfect your technique?"

I whispered in her ear, "Just you."

Her glazed eyes cleared a bit. "I'm the only one you've ever been with?"

"Wouldn't that make you feel high and mighty?" I brushed her ear with my nose. "I've never used my super-powers, like you call them, on anyone else before."

Her head shot up. "Seriously?"

I gave a little laugh. "Seriously."

"Fuck. You have no idea how much that turns me on."

Then she was attacking me with her mouth, her hands, her knee between my legs. Her nipples traced patterns against my chest and face. Amira thrust my arms and legs out wide until I was spread-eagled on her bed. I was naked and exposed, brimming with want. I watched her glide like a serpent down me. She watched me back. Amira flashed that crooked grin before pressing her lips to my lips.

Her tongue traced complicated shapes on my maze of folds, slowly searching deeper and deeper. With her deft tongue, she pulled back my hood. Pushing past all my secrets, she found the heart of me. The fire of her mouth spread to me. Flames licked at my clit.

There were no words, no thoughts. Only heat. Like a fish, I gulped in air, but it only scorched my lungs. At her mercy, I burned. Her tongue was a cruel mistress. Distantly I heard myself begging for more of her rough tongue with its power to strip away everything that wasn't this agony of pleasure.

I would have faced the fires of hell to keep her mouth on me like this for all eternity. But I wasn't that strong. My body quaked as the orgasm rushed through me. Like a tidal wave it quenched all that heat, leaving nothing in its wake but the smoky remains of desire.

I lay there spent, in a daze. When my eyes could focus again, I saw cracks on the walls. As I came around, Amira was standing at her broken windows, looking at the street down below. There were car alarms and sirens.

Fear descended on me. "What happened?"

When Amira turned to me, her eyes were round like

big, dark universes. "I think you broke the building."

"Oh no, no, no, no, no . . . " I stuttered.

Then she laughed. "I'm just fucking with you. It doesn't look that bad." She tiptoed her way back to bed around broken glass. "Looks like we had ourselves a little localized earthquake."

"No one's hurt?"

She shook her head. "My apartment took the brunt of it."

I hung my head. "I am so, so sorry."

Amira scoffed. "It's a rental. Be sorry all you want as long as we get to do *that* again."

Then I was back in her arms, and she was once again stoking the fires inside me.

Since then, I've become the one people turn to instead of turning to despair. I've made the earth and air tremble. I've changed land formations forever. I've fought in wars. I've saved lives. I've seduced women. But it all began, I began, with Amira and that night.

THE LADY INVENTORS'
CLUB OF KINK

Andrea Dale

My mistress is part of an elite club of women, all engineers and scientists and programmers. They share one other interest: lesbian BDSM, as creative as their wicked minds can make it.

To that end, they formed The Lady Inventors' Club of Kink. They challenge each other to invent ever more devious and torturous devices and toys, and hold quarterly parties to show them off.

Build a better mousetrap? Oh yes they can, especially when it comes to designing one that will snap cruelly on a sub's tender nipples without warning. Possibly by remote control.

The theme of tonight's party is Animals.

No actual, living animals will be a part of it, of course. Kink means consensual. Leather is allowed; real fur is not. But other than that, the theme is, as always, open to interpretation.

My mistress is hosting the party this time. Her estate is

outside Silicon Valley, in the hills, with a wall of windows affording breathtaking views of the glittering city below. The main floor is open plan with high, beamed ceilings, and tonight the furniture is arranged around the perimeter so that there's space for the demonstrations and displays.

Her housekeeper and chef have the night off; the hors d'oeuvres are made and the submissive girls will serve those and the drinks.

My job, of course, is to answer the door and usher the guests in.

I can greet the guests only with a polite bow and my hands extended for any coats, because my mistress has already fitted me with a bit gag. Other than the tasteless, brown silicone bit in my mouth, the rest of the gag is made of brown leather and chrome rings, and the rich smell of the leather fills my senses.

Soon I'll smell my own sweat and juices . . . if I'm lucky.

I know my mistress has been hard at work on her device for tonight. I'm aware, roughly, of what it's like, because she'd needed to fit it to my body. She likes to win in all things, including these party challenges, and that usually means a win for me.

In deference to the theme, my blonde hair is in two high pigtails, and a small, jaunty red cowboy hat perches between them. A Western shirt, white with red embroidery, skims my upper thighs; I'm not wearing anything underneath. My red cowboy boots click smartly on the slate entrance tiles.

Given all that, I'm guessing pony play is in my near future. While it's not my favorite variation, anything that involves bondage and teasing and a little pain excites me beyond belief. My pussy lips are already slick with moisture, my clit growing fat with erotic tension.

Many of the other subs are also erotically and inventively costumed, although some simply arrive naked. The gated estate is private, and the night is warm.

There's a cat girl in ears and whiskers and a black PVC bodysuit, which has cutouts for her nipples and crotch, as well as metal rings in various places—to bind her to something, to bind toys to her.

Another girl is wearing a long, elaborate black-and-yellow bird beak over her nose. Her eyes twinkle as she lifts her head so I can see beneath the beak. It's also a gag, and her mouth is smiling around it. Strategically placed feathers tickle her reddened, peaked nipples.

Yet another is wrapped in white gauze, only her eyes and nose visible. The bandages go down to her upper thighs, so she can walk to the house. There are some unusual lumps on her back, beneath the stretchy white fabric. She'll be fully mummified before the night is out, I imagine, but I wonder what that has to do with any animal.

When everyone has arrived, the games begin.

Some of the inventions had been delivered earlier, uncrated and assembled and covered with pristine white sheets. I've seen none of them, and I assume most of the subs haven't, either. Not every Lady Inventor created a large device, of course.

I was right about the girl wrapped in gauze. She lies on a large, padded table in the middle of the room, and her mistress continues wrapping gauze around her legs and around the table in various places, pinning her to the padding. The mistress explains that her sub is wearing a remote-control clit vibe, and then performs some breath play on her while adjusting the vibe controls. When the sub can't breathe, she quivers, her hips thrusting as she tries to come, but can't.

The mistress releases her, allowing her to stand. "Behold, from the chrysalis emerges the butterfly." She cuts the gauze away. Now we can all see a harness strapped to her back, the straps around her hips that hold the vibrator in place, and the sparkling, jeweled rings in her nipples.

The sub, sweaty but smiling, spreads her arms and grasps the upper bars of the X-frame on the wall. She doesn't need to be restrained; she obeys all commands. As her mistress paddles her, every time she arches her back, the motion triggers the harness. We watch in fascination as butterfly wings, lush with jewel-tone colors, grow with each jerk of her body. Finally her mistress turns the remote up to high and lets the sub come, and as she does, the giant wings flutter as if she were taking flight—and in some ways, with her grateful orgasm, she is.

The cat girl, her hands encased in paw-shaped mittens, is made to parade on hands and knees. Chains run from a belled collar around her neck to the clamps on her nipples, tugging the sensitized buds as she moves. When her mistress slides a butt-plug cat tail into her, she arches her back, pretending to knead the floor. Finally, she's made to stand, her wrists cuffed and attached to a hook in the ceiling, her stance widened with a spreader bar, her nipple clamps removed.

Now her mistress dons needle-sharp claws, which she grazes along the girl's flesh, making her gasp and wriggle. Then she traps the sub's nipples between the evil, pricking claws. Two more mistresses assist, one jiggling the butt plug while another presses a Hitachi wand to the sub's clit.

I know this sub. She loves to come, any time, any place, and usually can do so at her mistress's command—which her mistress now commands her to do. But I guess her predicament: when she comes, she will writhe and jerk, and those vicious claws will sink into her nipples, which are already tender from the clamps. It's horrifyingly amusing and arousing to watch her struggle to stay still while orgasming.

Then it's my turn.

Again, I have some vague ideas about my mistress's device, but she blindfolded me before finishing adjusting it to my body, so I had no idea what it looked like.

Or what it could do.

I knew it was something padded that I bent over, cradling my torso as I rested on my hands and knees. There were cutouts for my breasts to fit into, so they dangled down, easily reached, and there was some kind of additional, removable piece at the other end that supported a dildo but left my clit and ass otherwise accessible.

Now, I gasp around the bit in my mouth at the sight of the device. It is a beautiful, carved rocking horse, fashioned out of pale wood. My head will rest in a groove in its head. Its saddle is shaped from a soft, dark-brown leather cushion along its back.

Mistress has me remove my shirt and boots. Then she attaches blinders to my head, so like a racehorse, I can see only forward. I'm trembling with nerves and neediness by the time she says, "On you go, darling."

I drape myself over the horse, adjusting my breasts into the holes, settling myself until I'm comfortable. Of course, "comfort" is a tricky word in this type of situation.

Mistress doesn't want me unduly harmed, and wants me secure so that our scene can go on longer.

Once I'm ready, cuffs attached to the horse's legs near the bottom are strapped around my wrists. She places a buzzer in my right hand and assures me that I can press it in case of emergency, since I can't speak. Then Mistress moves behind me, where my spread legs rest along the outside of the horse's hind legs. She smooths a hand over my ass as if she were caressing a skittish horse's flank, and I make a snuffing noise, hoping that it's appropriately horse-like.

"Good girl," she coos, and I flushed with pleasure.

I hear some clicks and the sound of wood against wood; obviously she is affixing the extra piece. Then she says, "Raise your hips, darling," and I do, and when she tells me to lower them, I feel the tip of a dildo slide between my slick pussy lips. It doesn't go in as far as I want it to—just nestles inside, about halfway in, frustrating and tantalizing—and I can't stop clenching around it, as if I could draw it farther inside me with my vaginal muscles alone.

Mistress chuckles, buckles cuffs around my thighs, then tugs a strap around my waist so I can't hump my hips. The plaintive mewl I make sounds more like a kitten, as my bondage predicament settles into my brain.

I hate being restrained. I love being restrained. I hate being on display. I love being on display. I hate being teased, especially in front of onlookers. I hate being told I'm not allowed to come when I'm desperate to, and I especially hate having orgasms in front of everyone; that's humiliating. And I love all that, too, including, bizarrely, the humiliation. The dichotomy of everything is what fuels my submissiveness, and Mistress knows how to play off of it all.

I'm sure my juices are already dripping down the dildo, staining the wooden base. When Mistress reaches beneath to pluck at my nipples, she isn't surprised to find them crinkled and hard. I already knew they were, without looking; I can feel them throb in time with my neglected clit.

I wriggle a little at her touch, wanting more, harder, yes, please, even though I can barely move.

Mistress laughs softly again, and I hear another *thunk-click* of a lever of some sort. Then she reaches beneath again and rakes her fingernails across my sensitive buds.

This time, when I wriggle, the horse moves: it rocks a tiny bit, just like a rocking horse should.

A squeal escapes my lips—when the horse rocks, the dildo moves.

"Now she understands," my mistress says, addressing the assembled guests. "When the horse rocks forward, the dildo pulls almost all the way out. When the horse rocks backward, it thrusts all the way in. Thus."

She pushes on the horse, sending it into motion. I moan through the gag as the dildo fucks me, and moan again when, after a few back-and-forths, Mistress makes the horse still.

I'm already so aroused that I'm sure just a few more thrusts would give me my release. I'm also sure that won't happen for some time—or if it does, that still won't be the end of things.

Mistress comes around in front of me to show me what's in her hand, and my eyes widen. I moan, "No," around the bit, but the safety buzzer in my hand remains silent. I don't want this (do I?), but I can't refuse my beloved mistress.

I'd known as soon as she put the blinders and bit gag on me that pony play of some sort would be involved. But I'd allowed my brain to block out the truth, the obvious fact that where there were blinders and a bit, there would be a tail. Even when I'd watched the cat girl submit to the humiliation of her tail being eased deep into her rectum—her eyes closed, an expression of combined bliss and embarrassment on her face—I'd refused to think further, to connect the dots.

I can feel the heat rise in my cheeks as someone else—because Mistress is in front of me—drizzles lube on my asshole and then massages it in, first one finger, then two. Another mistress? A sub?

The tail is long and graceful, pale blond. The horse and I, we are a Palomino. The plug . . . I know better than to close my eyes and refuse to look at it. The plug isn't large, but it is flanged to stay in, and it isn't just the plug, it's the tail, too, and I tremble.

My mistress moves back behind me, and fucks me gently in the ass with the plug until I am open enough to accept it popping in. "Good girl," she says again, and rocks the horse back and forth, the dildo fucking me, as a reward.

Again, she stops too soon.

My heart pounds—every beat of it sends pulsing throbs through my nipples, my clit, my ass, even my cunt, which twitches, half-empty and fully needy.

"I'm sure you all want to inspect my invention," she says to the onlookers. "Let's have some champagne and hors d'oeuvres, and anyone who wants to try her out, can. You know the rules."

They are allowed to touch me anywhere. They are

allowed, with specific request, to paddle me or spank me. They are allowed to tease me mercilessly.

They are not allowed to let me come. Only she has that authority.

Meanwhile, I am on humiliating, horny display.

My nipples are pulled, pinched, twisted. The cat girl's mistress even catches them between those wicked needle claws. I hold my breath, my pussy fluttering helplessly around the part of the dildo inside me.

When I am spanked, the horse rocks, until I don't know whether I want the spanking and rocking and fucking to stop or continue.

I have no idea how long this goes on. I'm a mess of desperate desire, my thoughts jumbled, my body sensitized and focused.

Through the haze, I hear Mistress's voice again. "I think we've tortured our plaything enough tonight, don't you, ladies?" She leans down to me, kisses the tip of my nose, and says, "I'll get you started out of the gate, darling, but it'll be up to you to bring home the purse."

And with that, she pushes the rocking horse, gets it going at a good, strong clip, and then steps back. "Go."

I understand. Once I have that momentum, I can throw my body back and forth along with the horse, keeping it going. Can I continue long enough to fuck myself to orgasm? I have to . . .

Oh god. I'm struggling to come amidst the crowd, their oohs and ahhs and encouragement and commentary filling me with humiliation, which in turn spurs me on as if a jockey with spurs rides me.

I have no idea if I am whinnying like a horse or squealing like a pig or just keening with need.

I'm close, so close, and so desperate. I fling my body back and forth, fling the rocking horse back and forth as hard as I can to drive that dildo into me, to fuck myself with it. I can hear the wet squelches as it drives in and out of me.

Please . . .

When the pressure builds, I almost lose the rhythm. I balance on the fine line between needing to stay focused and needing to let go.

Then, in my mind's eye, I imagine a finish line before me, imagine I am a nose ahead in the race, and just need one last burst of speed.

As my mental body breaks the tape, my orgasm breaks.

For an impossibly long moment, I freeze, and then I am screaming through the bit and shuddering and helpless as the rocking and the dildo urge every final pulse out of me.

Mistress places a wreath of roses around my neck.

PROVE IT ON ME

Cara Patterson

The office is too hot, and the fan whirls with a *rat-a-tat*. It's too hot for a smoke, even with the window wedged high and the shutters brought low. The wallpaper peels down in strips, like a parcel half-unwrapped. The walls underneath are yellow. Smoke or water or both. Enough to keep the rates low.

Jack pushes her hair back from her brow.

It's too damned hot for making trouble, and as always, that's when trouble always comes knocking.

The stranger steps on in. He stops, like they always do, frowning. Jack knows she ain't no Sheba. In a suit, she passes, but with her smooth chin, she looks young as a kid.

"Are . . . are you Mr. Parker?"

She rises. "Jack Parker."

He says his name is Marshall. Jack surveys him. Fifties, solid, fine cut to his suit. Come from money, then, and with plenty to eat and drink. Another look catches cracked veins on his nose. Too much to drink.

She leans back in her seat. "So what brings you here?"

The man is sweating, sending his white shirt gray. "I'm told you're good at finding people."

Jack inclines her head. "It happens. Who you looking for?"

He pulls a beat-up photograph out of his pocket. "My daughter. She got in with a bad crowd, Mr. Parker. Gone two weeks ago now; she ran off. Took her things and disappeared."

Jack takes the photograph. She's a regular girl, plain-faced and fair with a button-down blouse. Like any good little poppa's girl.

"How old is she?"

"Going on nineteen and stubborn as a mule." He takes a kerchief out of his pocket and wipes his forehead. "I'm a good Christian man, Mr. Parker. I can't just sit by and let her go down that road."

Jack draws her notepad closer. "Tell me about her."

It's a story she's heard a hundred times. Once, it was her own: a girl looking for excitement who sees New York as an adventure and don't want to stay in the backside of nowhere forever.

Mr. Marshall's girl ain't come so far. She likes to mix with all sorts. That ain't proper enough for her pappy.

Jack closes her book. "I'll see what I can find out," she says.

"You'll bring her home?"

Jack rises from her seat. "Can't promise that, but if she can be found, I'll find her."

He gave her places his baby girl—Gracie —used to go to. He looked there, he said, but Jack knows it's easy to hide out some place you know, especially if your old man sticks out like a crooked nail.

Those are the first places she goes when the evening sets in. She pulls on her coat and hat, and takes the trolley uptown to Harlem.

Mr. Marshall said a lot, but Jack can read between the lines. He don't like black folk and he don't want his girl around the likes of them. The way Jack figures, Gracie Marshall can spend her time with whomever she damned well pleases.

She lights up a cigarette and walks the streets. Marshall didn't know what to look for, but Jack knows the signs, places where speakeasies are tucked away, hiding behind storefronts and apartment blocks.

Three bars are a bust. One of them, she shows around Gracie's picture. They know her, sure, but she don't come there no more. She moved on to bigger things. One of the fellas, grinning, says she's taken to watching Miss Gladys.

Jack don't go to Harlem all that often, but even she's heard of Miss Gladys: the big lady with the big voice and the white tux, working out of the Clam House on 133rd. Some people don't know if she's Sheik or Sheba. Jack has got a hell of a lot of respect for a dame like that.

It puts a new spin on Gracie Marshall, if she's living it up with Miss Gladys.

Jack heads that way. It's tucked right away, but if you know where to look, it ain't hard to see it. The Clam House has a name, and sure enough, can't miss the lavender crowd.

It don't take much to get in. The dame at the door looks Jack over and nods, like she's one of them. Maybe she is, in her way. Sure, she don't dress up to strut onstage, but she sure as hell is acting up a storm. She ain't a fella, never wanted to be one, but damned if it ain't a hell of a lot easier living in pants.

The speakeasy is already filling up. Jack takes it all in: fellas arm-in-arm with fellas, dames cosying up to other dames. Her cigarette's burning low and she realizes she's staring. Ain't like she hasn't considered her likings. Always kept 'em buttoned right down. Don't need no distraction.

She sees a dark head turn, sees the face from the photograph. Little Gracie Marshall ain't half so innocent as her old man said. She's sitting on a table, a glass of shine in one hand, cigarette in the other. Her hair is darker, shorter, and she's painted up her face, and damn, if she don't look like a Nickelodeon queen.

Jack's still staring when Gracie notices her. She ain't the little mouse of a girl anymore. She's all lit up, smiling. Jack knows she's in a world of trouble as Gracie slips down off of the table and struts toward her, skirts and hips swinging.

"Haven't seen you around before, mister," she says, eyes shining. "Like what you see?"

Jack stares at her, like a fox on the railroad track. She don't need the distraction, and she's good as done her job. "I'm Jack Parker." All the words fall out her mouth like oats out of a split sack. "Your pop sent me looking for you."

Just like that, the smile winks out.

"I think you better get going . . . mister. Peepers aren't welcome here."

Jack touches the brim of her hat. "Miss." She turns to go, then pauses. "I ain't gonna tell him where you are, Miss Gracie. He wants to know you're safe."

"Sure," Gracie Marshall snorts. "Get the hell out of here."

Jack leaves, but not without looking back. Gracie is standing, face like thunder. She's found her place and she don't want to leave. Jack can't fault her for that. Sometimes, people never find their place. If you find it, you got to keep it.

She gives it a couple of days. Makes it look like she had to go a ways to find the girl. Don't want to make it easy if he goes looking again.

Mr. Marshall ain't pleased with Jack when she tells him Gracie is staying put. He wants to fetch her home and knock some sense into her. Jack ain't surprised. He looks the kind to speak with his fists. Jack tells him to go screw himself. She ends up with a busted lip and a shiner before she knocks Marshall on his ass.

He don't pay her and cusses her out. Calls her all manner of unsavory things. He'd be worse, she knows, if he realized he was talking to a dame, especially a dame with some smoke in her.

"This isn't over!" he snarls. "I'm going to find my girl, with or without your help."

She figures Gracie should know.

Okay, sure, she wants to see those pretty eyes again, but Gracie should know. She takes the trolley up to Harlem again. Gracie must have friends, because she can feel people staring at her. She ignores it and heads right on in.

Gracie finds her this time. "What do you want?" she demands, grabbing Jack by the shoulder. Jack turns and Gracie's eyes go wide. "Geez. You get into a fight?"

Jack wonders how bad it looks. She didn't stop to check. "Your old man stopped by," she says. "He's still looking for you."

Gracie's fingers are against Jack's cheek and she swears like a sailor. "He did this to you?" Jack hesitates and then nods, and Gracie looks mad enough to spit tacks. She takes Jack's hand, and pulls her toward a table. "You should have put ice on it."

Jack snorts. "You think I got ice in my office?"

Gracie's red lips pull tight. "Stay here." She's back in a second with a glass of ice. She tips some into a napkin and then presses it to Jack's eye.

Jack lifts her hand up to hold it. "Thanks." She watches Gracie. The girl ain't meeting her eyes. She's looking at the bruises, frowning. She knows to put ice on it and that gives Jack a mess of ideas about why she don't want to go home. "You should stay here."

"What?" Gracie looks confused.

"Don't go back," Jack says. "You got friends here. It's safer."

Gracie picks up another piece of ice and gently presses it to Jack's busted lip. "I'm not going back. Not ever."

"Good."

One of the fellas brings them drinks. Gracie doesn't even look at him. She's looking right at Jack, like it's the first time she's ever seen her. "He was paying you to find me. How come you didn't tell him I was here?"

Jack's got a thousand reasons. She shrugs. "Girls like us gotta stick together."

Gracie's dark eyes are shining. She sits back on the edge of the table, and picks up the glasses. "Girls like us, huh?" She holds out a glass. It's cold against Jack's fingers. "So what's your story, *Jack*?"

Jack knocks back the drink. It burns like billy-o. "Like yours," she says. "Just with more pants."

Gracie laughs, throwing her head back. Her dark hair bounces on her shoulders, and her neck is pale as sugar. Jack's hand shakes around the glass. She didn't come looking for no complications, but she never spoke to a dame like Gracie before.

"You staying for the show?" Gracie asks.

Jack says no. Cases, she says, and she cuts and runs. She's three blocks away before she starts regretting it. Still, can't go back. Not tonight. Bad enough to skedaddle. Worse to come crawling back.

She gives it a day or two, until her face ain't so swelled up. She even gets herself a fine new tie. Don't hurt to smarten up once in a while. She's late for opening and when she slips in, Gracie's warming the crowd up.

She ain't got the greatest pipes, but she's got spunk. She's laughing and shaking her skirt with every kick. It's real short and her gams are as white as her neck. Jack's mouth is dry and she's staring.

Gracie spots her over the whooping crowd. She smiles and blows a kiss. Jack blushes like a schoolgirl. She heads to the bar and hides her face in a glass of shine. There's an empty table nearby and she's still sitting there when Gracie skips off the stage.

Jack don't have a chance to get up when all of a sudden Gracie is by the table. She steals Jack's glass and takes a mouthful, then sits right on down in Jack's lap, like it's regular. In this place, maybe it is. Jack still swears in surprise.

Gracie grins at her. Hers lips are red as Jack's tie. "I knew you'd be back."

Jack's heart beats like a drum. Gracie's face is close to hers, and Jack's breathing way too hard. She's straighter than this. She don't turn into a sap over a pretty pair of eyes. Not before, anyhow.

Still, she melts like butter in the sun when Gracie leans that little bit closer and kisses her right on the mouth. She ain't never been kissed by anyone, save Thomas Kelvin when she was ten. She decked him then, but she ain't got any plans to deck Gracie, not even when Gracie opens her mouth and licks at Jack's lips.

Jack gasps aloud, and her mouth is open, and Gracie's already slipping her tongue deeper. Jack's dizzy with it. She's pulling Gracie closer, and she can feel Gracie's fingers in her hair. She don't know where her hat is at.

She pulls back. Her lips feel all puffed out, and she's breathing like she ran a block. "Gracie . . . " It sounds like a prayer.

Gracie is smiling. Her fingertips touch Jack's lip. "Wanted to do that the other day, but you were all beat up."

"Sure," Jack snorts, looking away.

"Sure," Gracie retorts, lifting Jack's chin, making her look back at her. "You watched out for me. I like that in a fella, even when he isn't really a fella. Especially then."

"Ain't no Jasper," Jack mutters. True enough, she ain't a looker, but Gracie don't seem to care. Jack looks down again. Gracie's still in the skirt, and her legs are right there. Sweet Jesus, she wants to touch them, but that ain't a road she can let herself go down.

Gracie leans down and kisses the corner of her mouth. Jack closes her eyes, shivers. "I'm patient, Jack," she whispers. "You want me, you know where I am." She swings off Jack's lap and stoops to grab her hat. Jack swallows down a groan at the view. Gracie giggles, then sets Jack's hat back on her head. "Call it an offer."

Jack skips out again and this time, she can't deny she's running. Ain't till she gets back to her apartment that she sees the lipstick smudged on her lips. She stares at her reflection, heart drumming. She can remember Gracie's gams so clear. It don't take much imagination, and maybe it makes her a sap, but she lies on her bed fingering herself and thinks of Gracie like she ain't never thought of anyone before.

She wants to go back.

Next day, when the sun is high, and the fan is clattering, she thinks of ice on her lip and fingers in her hair. She'll go back and she knows it. She blows smoke at the ceiling and grins. Yeah. She'll go back and see if Gracie's in earnest. Hell, maybe just mack on her again.

The door rattles and she sits up sharp.

"Mr. Parker." It's Mr. Marshall, and he ain't alone. He got two bulls in uniform right behind him. "We need to have words."

Jack sits up straighter. Ain't right that he's brought the law into it. Of all the people in the room, he's the one who should be wearing the bracelets, 'specially now she knows what he did to his baby girl. "What's this about, Mr. Marshall?"

"You know damned well," Marshall snaps. "You know where my daughter is."

Jack rises, and she sees the way the cops look at her. She got her height and her big hands from her daddy, and none of them would ever guess she was anything but a fella. It makes her feel tougher. She leans on the desk. "Like I told you, Mr. Marshall, your daughter don't want to see you."

"Mr. Parker, the man has the right to see his daughter."

"And his daughter don't got the right to stay away from a man that beats on her?" Jack asks, raising her eyebrows. Marshall goes from red to white. "Mr. Marshall ain't no good gentleman. He beat on me, only three days back. I got no reason to tell him where his daughter is."

"I never . . . "

Jack knows she ain't gonna keep her temper, if he stays round much longer. "Mr. Marshall. I done a job for you, and you ain't paid me. You beat on me. Now, I want you to get the hell out of my office with these fine gentlemen, else I'm going to come down to the station myself and have charges laid on you."

He goes pale as milk. She knows he ain't got cause to charge her, but she sure as hell could see him closed up in the big house, even just for a day or two. He's too much of a chicken-liver to try his luck.

He storms out and the cops go too. Jack's hands are shaking. She reaches down into her drawer. She's got a bottle of bourbon there, half-empty. It's how she celebrates the end of a case, and that sure as hell was an end.

Half a glass drunk and she's still shaking. She ain't been caught yet, but with the law there, all it would take was an arrest and being checked in at the jail, and Jack Parker would be as good as dead. No matter how long she does it, all it'll take is one slipup.

Someone taps at the door.

"Yeah?"

The door opens a crack, and Jack's heart does a jump. Gracie.

She's on her feet in a second. "You shouldn't be here. Your old man . . . "

"I know," Gracie says. She closes the door behind her.

There's a deadbolt, and she pushes it closed. "He was in my part of town, asking questions again. Said he was going to see the no-good dick got what was coming to him."

Jack stares at her. "You come to warn me."

Gracie nods. "You don't need to get in trouble because of me."

Jack starts laughing. Maybe it's the relief. Maybe it's the giggle-juice. "Too late," she says, when Gracie looks lost. She grins. "He brought in the cops. Thought it'd scare me. I turned them on to him instead. He ran."

Gracie's eyes look bigger in the light of day. "He's gone?"

"Pretty sure for good, this time," Jack says. "Least-ways, he ain't coming after me, and if you want, we can shake him off of your tail too."

Gracie comes toward her. "You'd help me?"

Jack nods. "Sure." She's leaning down just as Gracie's rising on her toes, and they meet somewhere in the middle. Gracie's arms go around her neck and Jack pulls her closer. This time, she's the one licking at Gracie's mouth, until Gracie tastes like her bourbon too.

She don't know what gives her the thought, but she hitches Gracie up under her ass and sets her on the desk. Gracie giggles, leaning back.

"You got a lot of front, Mister Parker," she says, spreading her knees. Jack ain't one to ignore a welcome like that and steps right between them. Her hands bunch in Gracie's skirts, pushing them up, until stockings give way to warm, soft skin. Gracie's mouth is against hers again and she sucks soft on Jack's bottom lip. "You want to touch me?"

Jack squeezes her thighs. She's light-headed again, and

Gracie's teeth catch her lip. Jesus god, she's making Jack forget how to breathe.

"I ain't never . . . " Jack says, feeling like an ass. "This . . . I ain't . . . "

Gracie kisses the tip of her nose. "Want a suggestion?" Jack nods, and Gracie's mouth is suddenly warm against her ear, the breath sending shivers through her. "Sit down, and bring your chair in close."

Jack all but falls into her seat. She can see where this is going. When Gracie kicks off her shoes and her feet slide along the arms of the chair on either side of Jack, Jack swears to god her heart is gonna beat right out of her chest.

"Jesus god . . . " she whispers, as Gracie hikes her skirts up high. She ain't got any smalls on. As dark as her hair is on top, down there, it's all pale curls. Jack ain't seen anything like it before. Gracie is watching her, and biting her bottom lip. Jack looks up, breathless. "You'll let me . . . ?"

Gracie's eyes shine. "Please."

Jack's hands are still on Gracie's thighs. They're warm and soft, and Jack knows exactly what she wants to do. She drags the chair closer, wedging her foot under the wheel to keep it from skidding back, and presses her mouth to the top of Gracie's stocking. Gracie giggles and tilts her hips, and Jack has to catch her thighs with both hands to hold her still.

She can smell Gracie. Not the perfumed up-top Gracie, but the smell of her sex. Lord in heaven, Gracie wants, and she wants bad. Jack shivers and presses openmouthed kisses all along the bare skin, closer until curls brush her cheeks.

She don't know if it's right, but she sucks on the skin, right there, high up on Gracie's plump thigh. Gracie makes a sharp sound, and one hand is in Jack's hair. Not pulling her back, though. Pushing her closer.

Jack sucks again, hard enough to leave a mark, something to remind Gracie whose mouth was there. She lifts her head back, and it's like a red rose on that pale skin. She drags her tongue across it, and Gracie moans. Ain't much of a sound, but it goes right through Jack.

"Jack." Gracie's voice is breathless.

Jack smiles. Gracie knows what's what when it comes to stuff like this, but she ain't the one making anyone moan and pant like Gracie is right now. Jack turns her head, and Gracie's intimate parts are right there. Lord knows Jack knows how to manage those. Last night, she had practice enough. Ain't never done it from this side before, though.

She slides one hand up Gracie's thigh, then down, dragging her thumb slowly up, brushing damp curls aside. Gracie shivers, and Jack wonders just how much she'll allow. She leans closer, then kisses Gracie right there, like she would kiss her on the mouth. Light first, but when Gracie leans back on the desk and spreads her legs wider, Jack knows light kisses ain't for down there.

She remembers how Gracie licked her mouth, and slowly drags her tongue against Gracie's warm folds. Gracie's squirming, and Jack can taste her. She's wet and warm, and Jack knows what she's looking for, searching up with her tongue, until she finds the place that makes everything a hell of a lot better. And when she finds it, when she presses her tongue hard to it, Gracie's legs wrap over her shoulders and pull her closer.

Jack licks at her. Quick, then slow, hard, then soft,

change it up, make her squirm. She slips her other hand down under Gracie's thigh, holds her still, but slowly, slowly slides her thumb up. She sucks slow on that little knot, then slides her thumb right into Gracie, smooth as silk, and Gracie's heels pound at her back.

"Atta girl," Jack whispers, turning her head to kiss Gracie's thigh. Her mouth is tiring, so she lets her hands do the work for a second, her thumb sliding slick and slow and her fingertips flickering across the bud.

Gracie's propped on her elbows now. Her head is back, and she's flushed pink, her mouth open and wet. Small sounds are getting out, gasps, whimpers.

"Gracie," Jack murmurs, rubbing her cheek against Gracie's thigh. She feels like a wanton, and damn if it don't feel great. She waits till Gracie looks her right in the eye, and she draws out her thumb and pushes in two fingers, and puts her mouth back down.

Gracie stares at her, wide-eyed, panting, and Jack strokes with her fingers and her tongue, until Gracie's thighs are tight around Jack's ears, and her whole world turns into warm, soft skin and the taste and smell of Gracie. Gracie's small cries turn breathless, and she falls back on the desk, limp as a rag.

Jack draws her aching mouth back, and tilts her head to rest against Gracie's thigh. Her chin is wet, and she licks her lips. All she can taste is Gracie and bourbon.

Gracie strokes her fingers through Jack's hair. "I'm keeping you, Jack Parker," she murmurs. "You and that mouth."

Jack blushes against her thigh. "For sure?"

Gracie pushes herself up on her elbows. "Yes, ma'am." She reaches down and grabs Jack's tie, pulling her up.

"Come here." She tastes herself on Jack's tongue and starts working at the buttons of Jack's shirt.

Above them, the fan whirls with a lazy *rat-a-tat*.

EAT AT HOME

Louise Blaydon

"What the hell's taking you so long, eh? I could have swum to India and picked myself a cuppa in the time you've been in here." Mel's long arms went easily around Sarah's waist, the flat of her pelvis pressing up against the curve of Sarah's backside.

"It's been five minutes, Mel," Sarah said. "Had to boil the kettle first, didn't I?" Her tone was chiding, but Mel's hands were strong and warm on the spurs of her hip bones through the borrowed jeans (Mel's), and already, she could feel the heat skipping up her spine, the tingles that caught her up when Mel was close.

"It's been forever." Mel sounded disgruntled. She leaned in, and rubbed the tip of her nose against the bolt of Sarah's jaw. Sarah shivered at the hot breath on her neck, then the featherlight touch of Mel's lips.

"Mel . . . " Her hands moved automatically to cover Mel's, pressing lightly on the backs. She wanted to be strong, the sensible girl she'd been brought up to be, but already she doubted her capacity for it, to maintain her sanity when Mel touched her. What *was* it about Mel? She only had to look at Sarah to set her pulse pounding, fast in her throat and hard between her legs. One touch, fingers to the inside of Sarah's wrist or lips to the nape of her neck, and she'd be wet, aching, pelvis tense with the urge to thrust up against something. Mel's hand would do. Mel's thigh, Mel's mouth. Mel made her crazy, turned her into this wanton thing she wanted to be ashamed of, but could not.

Mel didn't believe in shame.

"Mmm?" A brush of lips to the soft skin behind Sarah's earlobe, and then another, this time damply open-mouthed. Mel's thumb traced a line down the spur of Sarah's hip bone, and Sarah felt it in a hot spasm between her thighs, a gush of wet want that made her gasp.

"Oh," Sarah said weakly, head lolling slightly in automatic response to Mel's touches, and Mel laughed, slid a hand down to cup Sarah between her legs, her palm warm and her grip firm.

"You weren't going to say we can't," Mel murmured against the curve of Sarah's throat, "were you?"

Sarah's breath hitched, and Mel pushed closer, her middle finger rubbing along the seam at the crotch of Sarah's jeans. Sarah swallowed, thighs clenching automatically, and Mel made an appreciative sound, pressed a kiss to the nape of Sarah's neck. "That's my girl."

She popped the button one-handed, a deft twist of the wrist and then a slow tug to part the stubborn teeth of the zip. Sarah shivered, and when Mel touched her through her damp knickers, she couldn't resist a whimper, hips bucking. Where Mel was concerned, *can't* was an impossibility. She

still couldn't remember quite how that had happened—
she'd managed to reach the age of eighteen without ever
looking twice at another woman like that, and even when
she'd first met Mel through a friend at one of the riverside
nightclubs, she hadn't exactly realized the draw between
them was anything like that. Mel cut an impressive figure,
with her long legs and the imperious nose and the way she
walked, elbows tucked in and chin lifted like one of the
guys in *West Side Story*. Later, Sarah found out that the
imperious expression was more to do with Mel's shortsightedness than anything else, but it didn't change the way she
responded to Mel's general aura, her overwhelming refusal
to take nonsense from anybody. She had drawn Sarah in
without either of them realizing how strong the pull of her
orbit had become, until one day in the soft afternoon light
of Sarah's room, magazines spread across their laps, Mel
had looked up all of a sudden, put a hand on Sarah's jaw,
and said, "Stop me, babe."

Her eyes had been soft and dark, all sincerity, and
Sarah had felt her throat close up—not with fear, but with
shock at how little any part of her wanted to say *stop*
if it meant another second without Mel's mouth on hers,
without Mel as close to her as she could get. Saying yes
to this would be taking a step beyond everything Sarah
had ever imagined her life would become, but that was
always the way with Mel: she made you want to run at
cliffs, freefall; made the solid hard ground of what had
gone before seem mundane to the point of despair.

Sarah had said nothing, of course, just lifted her chin,
and when Mel had kissed her, it had been like nothing on
earth, nothing like awkwardly necking with Andy Finn
behind the gym in senior year, all tongue and groping

hands. Kissing Mel had been like a fantasy of what kissing could be, and after that, there was no going back.

Behind her, now, Mel was shifting, too, hips rocking just slightly against the curve of Sarah's arse as she pressed with two fingers, circling slowly. Mel always got her like this, just the heat of her body making Sarah feel about to crawl out of her skin. "Come upstairs," Mel whispered. Another kiss to the back of Sarah's neck, clinging for a moment, and then a wet touch of tongue that made Sarah convulse with shivers.

"Why?" Sarah managed, though her voice shook and she knew why, how could she not? But there was something about the way Mel laughed at her pretended ignorance, and then the way Mel's hand twisted deftly until—oh—her fingers crooked down beneath the thin cotton of Sarah's underwear, delving into her wetness, grazing her bare clit.

"Well," Mel said, very reasonably, "I could always give you head in the kitchen, but I don't think your dad would think much of that."

Sarah's thighs slackened automatically, letting Mel's fingers slip a little deeper until the tips pushed shallowly inside of her, touching the sensitive place just at the entrance. Her breath was ragged, and Mel was so warm against her, the palm of Mel's hand bluntly working Sarah's clit while her fingers moved idly, and god, these damn tight jeans were a fucking encumbrance.

"Stop," Sarah managed with an effort, her fingers stilling Mel's hand at the wrist, and then, "Upstairs."

Mel's smile was smug at that, predatory, but it only made the urgency flare more hotly in Sarah's gut as Mel withdrew her hand and moved toward the stairs.

Mel stormed into the bedroom like an invading army seizing possession; Sarah followed obediently, the flutter-rush of her pulse in her throat holding back any protest. The door clicked shut, then the latch. Nobody was due to be home for hours yet, but they never dared take any chances.

"Off," Mel said, nodding toward Sarah's opened jeans. Her hands went to the buttons of her own, and Sarah moved immediately, tugging at the denim with inelegant haste. Elegance didn't seem to matter much when Sarah knew that the quicker she disentangled herself, the quicker she'd have Mel's warm weight between her thighs, Mel's clever mouth on her throat, and anyway, there was no ladylike way to get out of jeans, so it only wasted time to try. Jeans kicked aside, Sarah fell back on her elbows on the bed and Mel was on her in an instant in T-shirt and panties, shouldering in between her spread thighs.

Mel ground down against her immediately, braced on her arms over Sarah's body, hips rolling in a firm, steady motion that pressed their cunts flush together, the cotton of their underwear damp between. Mel's strong hand cupped the back of Sarah's head and Sarah let herself be guided, lay down the rest of the way, and opened her mouth to Mel's, their tongues stroking restlessly over each other.

It was always startling to Sarah that Mel, with her sharp features and sharper tongue, should pay such thorough and enthusiastic attention to kissing. Tough boys didn't like kissing much, as everyone knew, and in every other way, Mel might have been as tough as any boy Sarah had ever come across. But her kisses . . . Sarah was helpless the moment Mel's mouth touched hers, the soft, searching touches of Mel's tongue to the smooth inside of her cheeks and the ridges of her soft palate pounding through her in waves of heat. By the time Mel ducked her head to nuzzle at the underside of Sarah's jaw, they were rutting against each other in earnest, fingers digging bruise-hard into each other's hips, the pressure building up fiercely between Sarah's legs.

"Fuck," she murmured, the word still strange and adult in her mouth. She threaded her fingers into Mel's hair, and rolled her hips up hard against Mel's just for the satisfaction of hearing her breath stutter. She could feel the long muscles clenching and lengthening in Mel's thighs as she moved, could feel the soft weight of Mel's breasts against hers, but still there was too much between them. She tugged at the collar of Mel's T-shirt. "Mel . . . "

"Yeah." Mel braced herself on one hand, the other fumbling messily with the back of her shirt, ruching up the fabric at the nape of her neck as she awkwardly hauled it upward. Sarah reached a hand to help, and between them they got it over Mel's head and off. Then Mel was down again, mouthing at the tendon in Sarah's throat, and Sarah felt the tingle all the way into her fingertips as she snapped the clasp of Mel's bra. It slipped forward, and Mel shrugged it aside impatiently, the ripple of her shoulders catlike, drawing Sarah's hands. Mel was all shoulder blades in this position, and Sarah's fingers found an obvious hold on her upper back, feeling the shift of muscles as Mel's kisses dipped lower, finding the hollow of Sarah's throat, the ridge of her collarbone. By the time Mel set to work on the buttons of her blouse, Sarah's head was thrown back, her breaths coming short and hard. Mel was quick, spreading the blouse open in a matter of seconds, and Sarah let herself be lifted, let Mel strip her of the blouse and undo the catch of her cumbersome bra. The next thing she knew, Mel had one of her breasts in each hand, pebbled nipples caught between her fingers, and Sarah groaned low in her throat.

Mel half laughed, and moved up over her so their mouths could catch and part again. Sarah felt the drag of Mel's nipples against her bare skin, and reached between their bodies to squeeze the soft heaviness of her breasts.

"Mmm." Mel broke away, panting, and Sarah was pleased to note the pinkness of her mouth, kiss-bitten, and the wild heat in her eyes. When she shifted downward, Sarah whined faintly in protest, but then Mel's mouth was hot and firm around Sarah's nipple, her knuckles offering a welcome pressure between her legs, and, yes, Sarah wanted that.

She rolled her hips up, rutting against the firm ridges of Mel's knuckles, but Mel was an unfair and horrible tease and the warm hand kept withdrawing, just slightly, and then dipping again, grinding just too lightly while Mel's mouth traced the underside of Sarah's breast, then the center of her breastbone. This was Mel's way, the withdraw and retreat, teasing until Sarah's legs were shaking and her back was arching restlessly off the bed, but Mel looked restless enough herself, and Sarah wasn't much in the mood for waiting.

"Mel, come *on*." The muscles in Mel's shoulders flexed under her palms, and then the hot amber gaze darted up toward her, half laughing.

"You pushin' me around, Sarah?"

Sarah lifted her chin defiantly. She could feel Mel's breath warm in the dip of her navel now, setting goose pimples rising on her thighs, and she was *so close* to where Sarah wanted her; so close.

And yet not close enough. "Yes," Sarah said, cupping a hand around the back of Mel's skull and canting her hips upward. "Get to it."

The ragged breath Mel drew through her teeth was more than reward enough for Sarah's bluntness; she didn't miss the way Mel's eyes closed momentarily as she ducked her head and pressed the flat of her cheek hard against the place where Sarah's dampness had seeped through the cotton of her underwear. It was a strange sort of pressure, this; at once diffuse and direct. Sarah groaned, and Mel groaned too, turned her face, mouth open. Sarah felt herself clench, cunt fluttering emptily around nothing at the sensation of Mel's warm breath against her, and then Mel's tongue, its heat blunted by a layer of cotton.

"Oh Jesus," Sarah managed, clutching at Mel's hair, and Mel must have been gone, because there was no smart-arse remark in return, just a sudden coolness as Mel lifted her face and hooked her fingers in the waistband of Sarah's panties.

The coolness was only momentary. A heartbeat later, Mel was settled between Sarah's legs again, all long black and soft hair fallen forward to skim Sarah's thighs. Her hands slipped underneath, strong and certain, lifting, and then her mouth slid hot and open between Sarah's parted thighs in the sweetest kind of kiss. Sarah whimpered, pelvis tilting upward automatically, and Mel moved with it easily, the flat of her tongue working in broad strokes through wet heat until it found the source, and dipped inside.

When she touched herself, Sarah didn't often bother

with anything other than firm, easy strokes to the clit. But with Mel—when Mel worked her up and teased her into submission like this—there was something about it that was everything Sarah wanted, everything she needed. Mel's tongue, at first, fucking shallowly, finding some strange secret place just inside Sarah's body that seemed to light her up everywhere, and then Mel's fingers, crooking inward when her tongue retreated, filling up everything that felt like an aching, empty space. Sarah was shivering, now, the muscles fluttering in her thighs, but Mel was nosing at her clit and flickering her tongue against it and they were both groaning, Mel's hips working helplessly down against the mattress as Sarah ground up against her face.

"Oh, fuck, oh Christ, oh fuck—"

Mel was proud of that, of teaching little Sarah to swear; but Sarah had never quite known the value of the words until Mel had fucked her hard enough to shake them out of her. Now, like this, Sarah was shaking, Mel's clever fingers slicking in and out of her, her mouth finding purchase on Sarah's clit and *sucking*, sucking, sucking. Mel always held off with that until Sarah was close like this, until her hips were jerking and her belly was spasming and her thighs were lifting shakily around Mel's shoulders; until she was arching her back and keening and her cunt clutching at Mel's fingers and oh fuck oh fuck Mel's *mouth*, finding her right where everything was building, right where she needed—

It burst up and out of her, as always, like a fucking exorcism. Between her thighs, Mel was shivering too, moaning and mouthing at her until the spasm passed and Sarah could fall onto her back again, part her legs. Mel withdrew her hand slowly, looking dazed, and Sarah felt a snarled pulse of gratitude and muted want.

"Jesus Christ." Mel's voice was strained, almost reverent; her fingers were slick and shimmered in the afternoon light as Mel put them to her mouth, withdrew them clean. Sarah groaned.

"Gimme a second."

"Second for what?" Mel threw herself onto the bed like a skein of silk, all long and elegant and gorgeous. Her thighs parted easily and without shame, her fingers slipping between.

Sarah's pulse was still thundering like a steam train, but she couldn't resist. "Oh, give over." She pulled herself up onto her elbow, propped over Mel, and her left hand tracked its way down Mel's flat belly, lower. Mel smiled slowly up at her, and withdrew her hand.

"Oh, I see," she said softly. "All yours."

"It better be," Sarah said.

Mel opened her mouth as if to respond, but Sarah was faster, her mouth catching at Mel's as her fingers slid into her wetness, finding her easily, circling. Mel groaned against Sarah's lips, arched her back, and god, yes, she must have been touching herself already because Sarah could already tell that she was close. That thought sent a wayward flush of heat through Sarah's stomach and her fingers stuttered, then picked up pace, her tongue rubbing hotly against Mel's. Mel shivered, seized up, as she always did just before, and that was Sarah's cue to keep going, to keep on kissing Mel's slack breathless mouth and rubbing at her clit until Mel's thighs flew up and clamped around Sarah's hand, stilling it abruptly as she came.

Afterward, Mel always looked curiously innocent,

something sleepy and childlike about her eyes. Probably, it was partly shortsightedness, but Sarah felt fond, still, looking up and seeing that. Mel's smile was fond, too, and the arm she reached out shakily for Sarah.

"Hey," she said, in that slightly coarse, sex-roughened voice that Sarah so loved. It sounded like Mel after a night on the town, belting out rock 'n' rollers into the karaoke machine; it sounded like them. As a child, Sarah had always imagined growing up to marry some guy she met in college, maybe; they'd have two kids and buy a house, get a dog. Everything was all planned out. It hadn't been until Mel that she'd realized it had all been planned out *for* her, and that things didn't actually have to be that way. That deviating from the plan someone else wrote out for you was frightening, but that scarier still was the thought that she might never have known she was being controlled at all, however benevolently. Mel made fear of the unknown into something Sarah wanted to dive headfirst into, because Mel would be there, and she made Life Before Understanding look like the ugliest cage in the world.

"Come here," Mel said, tugging Sarah's head down onto her shoulder, and Sarah went without resistance, seeing no reason not to. They were a team, she and Mel, a good team. And they'd only get better.

THE TRUTH ABOUT TARA

Annabeth Leong

What if all of it is true? You don't seem to have considered that. What if Tara lied about who she is, but what if I also saw right into her soul from the very first moment?

You want her to be so simple, a cackling villain, gun tucked into her purse, mask covering her face, blood caught underneath red nails. For some reason, you want to believe that a person like that could have fooled me, that I could have loved her if she had been so obvious and so cruel.

And you want me to be a fool, don't you? That's what this charade of yours is all about, isn't it? You think I don't know my rights? I am an American citizen. This is a domestic flight. I have a lawyer. You can't hold me. Are you charging me with a crime? You people might be working to change this stuff, but last I checked, habeas corpus still applies to those of us with blue passports.

I was on my knees licking Tara's pussy before I knew her name. Don't get wide-eyed. That's not an exaggeration.

I was working this noodle shop deep in the guts of the Venetian—yes, I originally went to Vegas to be a stripper, but the pole's not easy on the back, and that's only *one* of the ways I'm not as young as I used to be.

Anyway, she came through with a purpose. Nothing caught her eye, not the lights or the machines or the women. She looked like a dancer on an Alvin Ailey poster, long neck, long arms, dark skin, chin just so. I thought at first that she was hungry and searching for a meal that cost less than ten dollars. The people who go to the trouble to find that noodle shop are usually either Asians nostalgic for a taste of home or unlucky gamblers desperate to escape the fifty-dollar buffets. Some of those people come up to me with the same single-minded focus Tara had, and then ask for the chili oil cucumber and the Singapore noodles.

Tara walked up and didn't say anything. She just stood too close and looked at me like she knew every secret I ever told my best friend in middle school. She was older than I'd thought at first. Signs of age had gathered at the corners of her eyes and mouth. I liked that. I saw sadness in her, but also humor.

I remember she smelled cleaner than anything ever does in Vegas. No trace of cigarette smoke. No scents of any kind lingering from the night before. I wondered how it was possible—I haven't smoked since '96, but just walking through the casino floor to get to the noodle shop makes me smell like an ashtray and deposits a layer of soot on the inside of my lungs.

There weren't any other customers, so we stood that way much longer than normal, taking each other in. When I cleared my throat to ask if I could help her, it felt like I hadn't spoken in fifty years.

She smiled, brushed aside the order pad I'd lifted, and let her fingers rest on my arm. "I think you can," she said, and kissed me.

It was the sort of thing that happens in movies about Vegas, but I'd had years of living there to teach me not to expect something like that to happen to me. So when I opened my mouth, it was mostly out of surprise, but when she took that as an invitation for her tongue, I gave in to the moment all the way.

I'm not going to say she was a perfect kisser. She was in a bit too much of a hurry, and the sloppiness in her movements told me she wasn't as confident as she pretended to be. It's hard to explain, though, how flattering it is for someone as hot as Tara to seem so eager for *your* body, especially in Vegas, where it's clear every time you walk outside that your body isn't all that exciting in context.

I don't make myself up pretty like I used to when I was dancing. I've flirted with going butch, but I haven't mastered the swagger or the dapper look or the muscle. I feel just normal all the time—flat faced, flat assed, flat chested, too thick for androgynous glam looks, too small to really take up space—and in Vegas, feeling normal means feeling drab.

So when she kissed me with her need way out ahead of her finesse, I melted for her. I put the order pad down on the counter, then used that newly freed hand to grab Tara's ass. I checked to make sure the register was locked, then steered us toward the switches in the back. I turned off all the lights, but most especially the open sign. I tried to do all this without letting up on kissing her, as if she'd disappear if our mouths separated. I probably thought she would, but the way I was moving made her giggle, and I finally had to pull back.

I held her upper arms in my hands, squeezed as hard as I dared, and looked into complicated brown and hazel eyes. "Stay here for one sec," I said, meaning for it to come out as a command but making it sound like a question. She giggled again, and I rushed over to the cooktop so I could make sure a grease fire wouldn't interrupt whatever we were about to do together.

The whole time, my head kept twisting around to look at her, and that meant I noticed on some level—nothing conscious until I thought about it later—that there was a commotion of some sort out on the casino floor. Maybe I even guessed, in some buried part of my mind, that there had to be a reason for this woman's appearance and her sudden interest in me, and that the glimpses I caught of uniformed personnel—hotel security, but also police and also FBI—might go some way toward explaining my unusual good fortune.

You have to understand, though, that none of these thoughts broke the surface while my lips were tingling from her minty lip gloss and my ears were ringing with suggestions I was trying to get up the courage to make to her. Wondering who she was and where she'd come from—that stuff came later, alone in my bed, shivering in skin that still wanted to be heated by her touch.

Right then, that day, I rushed back to her as quickly as I could and asked if she wanted to join me in the private employee closet. And she did. She very much did.

You want to know what happened in the closet? If she was trying to hide out in there, she wasn't quiet about it.

As soon as I closed the door behind us, she slammed me up against it and took off my clothes like she was angry at them for keeping me from her for so long. I needed her naked, too, but I was clumsier about it, so mostly I made her look messy—one breast bare, the other covered, skirt half-off, panty hose down just enough for me to get my hand inside her panties.

I wanted to fuck her harder than my muscles could handle, and any other time I would have backed off, but this time I discovered that if you grunt and pant you can squeeze out a little more effort.

So we weren't at all quiet, no, and it didn't seem to me like we were trying to be. My wrist and forearm burned, but I wasn't about to let anything stop me from shoving my fingers into her. She kissed me like she wanted to swallow me. When she reached between my legs, I spread wide so she could get to me whatever way she wanted, and I knocked over a stack of boxes in the process, and I did not give a flying fuck.

Shit was crashing everywhere, and our bodies were dusty from the closet and sweaty from what we were doing and fragrant from how wet we were, and I felt awkward but sexy, and she was just everything to me right then. When you're living out a fantasy you never quite admitted you had, you don't stop or slow down. You grab as much of it as you can. You're greedy as hell for it. You'll do anything to keep it from escaping.

So I felt her come around my hand, and she looked so fucking gorgeous, head flung back, shoulders shuddering, one hand flung out to the side like she needed it for balance and the other pushing into me. She seemed impossible, and I got nervous she'd be done after the orgasm faded, that she wouldn't want to do me in return, so before she could recover I got free of her grip, sank to my knees in front of her, and buried my face in her cunt.

I enjoyed one glorious taste of her. She was dripping like a candy bar left out in the sun, all over my tongue, all over my face. If nothing had interrupted us, I might have stayed right there until I got fired, but yeah, that was the moment someone banged on the door to the employee closet.

She went stiff, but so did I. I didn't think anything of that. Seemed like a natural response to getting caught fucking a stranger. I jerked my head away from her clit and called out, "Yeah?" I was so hopped up and aroused, it didn't even occur to me to pray the person on the other side wouldn't turn out to be my boss.

"FBI. Would you mind if we open this door and look inside?"

I freaked out. Not because I had anything criminal to hide, but because it was embarrassing. How could this happen to me the one time I did something wild and sexy? "Um, I actually do mind," I called back. Both of us inside the closet were getting ourselves put back together, but no matter how put together I could get, I had no desire for a walk of shame in front of federal agents.

There was shuffling outside the door, but no one tried the handle. After a little while, the agent on the other side said, "Mind if I ask who's in there with you?"

I glanced at the woman in the closet with me and realized I'd never asked her name. I felt the blush heating my chest and sort of wanted to hide in there for the rest of my life. "My girlfriend," I said.

"Have you known her long?"

"Yes?"

I didn't regret what I'd been doing, but I also felt weird admitting the full extent of it to some guy through a door.

There was more commotion and some conversation I couldn't hear, but then a second voice spoke, loudly. "Jesus, Neil, don't be a perv. You can learn about lesbian sex when you're off duty. Leave the poor woman alone."

"Thanks for your time," the first voice said. The man's palm tapped the door as if patting me on the shoulder by proxy. "Um, carry on."

Carry on? God, we cracked up. I laughed until I couldn't breathe and my stomach cramped. Then I looked at her and said, "I really ought to have found out your name, like, before."

She said her name was Tara McCready and that she was in town for a conference for medical device manufacturers, and in no way did I think to question her because she kissed me after that. We shoved enough things aside to just lie down on the closet floor. She put her thigh between mine and grinned, and I had a roaring sensation in my chest, like I was a fire and she was my fuel, because that was the moment I knew she wasn't leaving anytime soon.

I've never had anyone touch me like Tara did. What she could do with teeth and tongue and fingers . . . Pleasure was a stunning force when it came from her. I couldn't move. I couldn't think. There was grime from who knows how many years grinding into my back, but I didn't care.

I came until I didn't think I wanted to anymore, but she kept finding ways to start me up again. We had to have been in that closet for hours. I'd never been that sweaty, that dirty, that sexy—and I've never cared that little about how I looked.

We stumbled out eventually. If we'd come out sooner,

I might not have asked, but after all that time, I'd gotten a little bit used to getting what I wanted. "Tara," I said. "My apartment's not far. I don't know how long you're in town, but . . . "

She kissed me, slow and sensual, but I could also feel a new distance between us. "Actually," she said, "I've got to be on a plane out really soon."

"Oh," I said. Tears sprang to my eyes, and they made me feel greedy.

Her face softened at the sight of them. She touched my cheek. "This was fun," she said, "but it wasn't just fun. I needed that, more than you know." She had me write my number down on a length of receipt paper for her—she said she'd forgotten her phone in her hotel room. "I'll be in touch," she said, "if I'm back in town. If it's okay with you . . . I think I will be."

Yes, later I saw things on the news. I made some guesses based on them. And, yes, when I Googled her later, I found out that Tara McCready didn't work for any medical device manufacturer that I could find, so I knew she'd told me some lies. But I didn't think her body had lied to me, and I didn't think she'd lied when she said she'd find her way back. Maybe she needed more than a good lay, but don't we all?

I saw her a lot for a while. You've probably got security camera footage of us together in every casino in Vegas. We weren't high rollers. She'd take me out for nice dinners, and then maybe we'd play a few hands of blackjack or low-stakes poker or sometimes catch a show before going back to my place. She never did anything that forced me to ask questions. She spent the sort of money on me that a corporate drone traveling on an expense account can spend.

Honestly, what we had was about the sex. Anything we did beforehand was a sort of foreplay in itself, a way of teasing each other until it was time to go to bed.

One time, she took me to a rodeo, and it took me a while to figure out why she kept saying the word in a funny way, emphasizing the O at the end, drawing it out into this orgasmic *ohhhh*. It didn't make sense until later in the evening, when she pulled down her waistband and I saw the top of her RodeoH harness.

Am I making you uncomfortable? I thought you wanted all the details. What do I know? Maybe her favorite brand of strap-on harness would help you identify her in a search. Maybe you could find it in her luggage.

It wasn't all about the sex. No. I meant that thing I said at first about seeing into Tara's soul from the first moment.

What I saw isn't something I can describe to you. I recognized her. I liked her. I wanted her. I knew she would be good for me. And she was. Best thing that ever happened. It wasn't just that hot time I told you about. It's like I walk differently for days after I've been with her. Don't get that look about it. I'm not talking about thighs worn out from too much sex. I mean I hold my head up. I look people in the eye. She loves me in this way that makes me feel like I'm someone worth loving, and I've never had that before.

She's a complicated person, like anyone else. She has weird habits—she likes to eat plain pasta noodles with her hands. She tosses and turns in her sleep. She pulls up YouTube videos of stingrays before bed because she says it relaxes her.

And there's things maybe you would say about her. Organized crime? I'm not saying that. You are. Stolen money? You again. Hardened criminal? I don't believe that. There's nothing hard about her. I don't know what makes you think I'd rat her out. As far as I'm concerned, she didn't abandon me. She just hasn't called me yet. And no, that's not an invitation for you to watch me until she does.

Okay, yeah, that's footage of us having a fight. It's the last time you caught us on camera in Vegas, and that makes sense, because it was the last time I saw her.

FROM A VOICE ON A TAPE: "We're partners or we're not, Tara. You tell me who you are. You tell me what you're up to. You keep me by your side from now on, or you can forget about all of this. This whole thing has gone too far for me to sit here and wait by the phone for you. My apartment's not a vacation spot. I love you, damn it!"

I've got no comment on that.

What's in Iowa? Camping. Trails. Wineries. A writing program. Cornfields. The Clinton LumberKings. People. What do you want me to say?

What am I doing there? It's an insult to the state to suggest there's no reason to go to Iowa on vacation. You searched my bags. You saw the climbing shoes, the tent, and all the rest of my gear.

Will that be all? My lawyer just texted. She says you definitely can't hold me here any longer unless you're charging me with a crime. Are you?

You look so disappointed. I haven't told you a single lie. Yes, I'm going camping and climbing. Yes, I still love Tara, and I know she loves me. You can believe whatever you want to, but I don't think you'll catch her. Not even if she was meeting me in Iowa. Not even then.

Now, if you'll excuse me, I have a plane to catch.

ABOUT THE AUTHORS

M. BIRDS is a writer and musician from Vancouver, British Columbia. Her short fiction has previously been published by Freaky Fountain Press, Cleis Press, and Hot Ink Press.

LOUISE BLAYDON is a writer and academic who loves cats too much. She has published a number of novels and many short stories with both f/f and m/m pairings. She lives in England with an ever-increasing number of pets.

EMILY L. BYRNE's (writeremilylbyrne.blogspot.com) stories have appeared in *Bossier, Spy Games, Forbidden Fruit, First, Summer Love, Best Lesbian Erotica 20th Anniversary Edition, Witches, Princesses and Women at Arms,* and *The Nobilis Erotica Podcast.* Her collection, *Knife's Edge: Kinky Lesbian Erotica* is available from Queen of Swords Press.

ANDREA DALE's (AndreaDaleAuthor.com) work— which has been hailed as "poignantly erotic," "heart-breaking," and "exceptional"—has appeared in twenty years' best volumes and about a hundred other anthologies from Soul's Road Press, Harlequin Spice, and Cleis Press. Her latest novella is *Kiss on Her List*.

HEATHER DAY (Twitter @heatherxday) has been writing erotic fiction since 2009, reading it for longer still, and has always been partial to a sexy superhero. Her stories can be found nestled in other Cleis anthologies such as *Girl Fever* and in *The Xcite Book of Lesbian Romance*.

NANISI BARRETT D'ARNUK, known mainly as a conductor and jazz pianist, holds the distinction of being the first open lesbian to conduct on the stage of DAR. Constitution Hall in Washington DC She is known mainly for her Cameron Andrews Mystery series.

ROSE DE FER's stories appear in *Best Lesbian Erotica, Best Women's Erotica, The Mammoth Book of Erotic Romance & Domination, Hungry for More, The Big Book of Submission, Red Velvet and Absinthe, Darker Edge of Desire, A Princess Bound,* and numerous Mischief anthologies including *Underworlds* and *Submission*. She lives in England.

SARAH FONSECA's (girlsinmitsouko.tumblr.com) essays, criticism, filthy ideas, and overlapping iterations have appeared in publications including *Autostraddle, Buzzfeed, Math Magazine, Nylon Magazine, A Quiet Courage,* and *Sinister Wisdom*. A Southern state expatriate, Fonseca also blogs and obsesses over Eartha Kitt.

DENA HANKINS (denahankins.net) writes aboard her boat, preferably in a quiet anchorage. Previously a sex educator, she writes erotica and romances spanning the queer alphabet. Her novels—*Lysistrata Cove, Heart of the Liliko'i,* and *Blue Water Dreams*—are erotic romance with queer and trans leads.

THEDA HUDSON's steamy erotica presses the boundaries of sex in *Best Lesbian Erotica 2011* & *2015, Best Lesbian Romance 2011* & *2012, Best Women's Erotica of the Year, Volume 1,* and her contemporary erotic fairy-tale novel, *Dyke Valiant.*

VICTORIA JANSSEN's (victoriajanssen.com) *The Duke and the Pirate Queen* is set in the same universe as her first novel, *The Duchess, Her Maid, The Groom and Their Lover,* which might be the only Harlequin featuring a sex scene with eunuchs.

ANNABETH LEONG (Twitter @AnnabethLeong) is frequently confused about her sexuality but enjoys searching for answers. She is the author of *Untouched* and the short-story collection *Liquid Longing,* and the editor of *MakerSex: Erotic Stories of Geeks, Hackers, and DIY Projects.*

CARA PATTERSON is a Scottish writer who has been writing since she learned her letters. She has a particular weakness for historical fiction and continues her love-hate relationship with in-depth international historical research.

JANELLE RESTON (janellereston.com) is a pansexual powerhouse who loves watching the *X-Files* and making sexual innuendos. Her erotica and romances have appeared in numerous anthologies. She lives in a northern lake town with her partner and their black cats.

AMANDA RODRIGUEZ is a queer, first-generation Cuban-American and an environmental activist living in North Carolina. She holds an MFA from Queens University in Charlotte. Her writing can be found in *Germ Magazine*, *Pine Mountain Sand & Gravel*, *Mud Season Review*, *Rigorous*, and *Stoneboat Literary Journal*.

PASCAL SCOTT is the pseudonym of a Decatur, Georgia–based writer whose work has appeared in *Harrington Lesbian Literary Quarterly*; *Thunder of War, Lightning of Desire*; *Through the Hourglass: Lesbian Historical Romance*; *Order Up: A Menu of Lesbian Romance and Erotica*; and *Unspeakably Erotic: Lesbian Kink*. Her first novel, *Hard Limits*, was recently published by Blackout Books.

A. D. SONG is a femme dyke who can be found in her natural habitat of used bookstores and bakeries. She is a writer, an artist, and a professional tease. Her inspirations include her community, kink, and one particular whip-wielding butch.

ANNA WATSON queers the suburbs west of Boston and loves to take part in a good anthology like this one, or *Me and My Boi, Best Lesbian Erotica 2015, No Safewords, Sometimes She Lets Me*, and their ilk. A recent venture is Laz-E-Femme Press.

ABOUT THE EDITOR

SACCHI GREEN (sacchi-green.blogspot.com, facebook.com/sacchi.green) is a Lambda Award–winning editor and writer who lives in western Massachusetts, retreats to the mountains of New Hampshire whenever possible, and makes occasional forays into the real world. Her work appears in scores of books, including nine editions of *Best Lesbian Erotica*, and she's edited fourteen anthologies, including *Best Lesbian Erotica of the Year: 20th Anniversary Edition*.